MR. MAYBE RIGHT FOR HER

COWBOY CONFESSIONS, BOOK #2

JO GRAFFORD

Mr. Maybe Right for Her

Copyright © 2022 by Jo Grafford

Cover design: Jo Grafford of JG PRESS

ISBN: 978-1-63907-039-8

ACKNOWLEDGMENTS

Many, many thanks to my editor, Cathleen Weaver, for helping me polish this story and make it the best it could be. I also appreciate my super awesome beta readers — Debbie Turner, Mahasani, and Pigchevy. I want to give another shout out to my Cuppa Jo Readers on Facebook. Thank you for reading and loving my books!

CHAPTER 1: THE NERVE OF HER!

BELDON

WHAT IS SHE DOING HERE?

Beldon Cassidy's heart ached with a special brand of anticipation at the sight of Jade Arletta's car parked in front of the big red barn that housed his family's store. Only a small amount of the sparkling emerald paint was showing beneath the amount of snow clinging to its hood. He was surprised that she'd driven her Jaguar in this weather. No doubt the unpredictable and infuriating woman had her reasons, ones he probably wasn't going to like.

Which didn't make him any less anxious to see her again. Though he'd been purposefully avoiding his oldest brother's ex-girlfriend, a part of him never stopped longing to bump into her again. It was a feeling that kept surfacing, no matter how deep he tried to bury it.

If he was a better man, he would've turned his pickup truck around and headed home. Instead, he drove doggedly closer to the one woman in the world he wanted, but couldn't have.

The chains on his snow tires churned through the snow that was swiftly blanketing the road with a fresh layer of whiteness. The outside temperatures had been too cold to melt the snow from the last storm two days earlier. It had been packed down by vehicles into an icy bottom layer, making the road particularly treacherous this evening.

Which begged the question: How in the world had their diva neighbor from the ranch next door managed to make it up the low-rise hill to Cassidy Farm in her luxury roadster? The feat must have taken every ounce of her bulldog determination.

As Beldon pulled into the parking spot next to hers, he noted her car had neither snow tires nor chains, and her hubcaps were half buried in the icy fluff. She'd been parked there awhile.

A burst of fear shot across his tongue at the possibility that she'd become injured. Or sick. In which case, his mother and brothers could probably use an extra set of hands right now. The thought that he might be needed inside the store made him feel a little less guilty about not turning around and driving away.

Though he'd spent all day herding cattle across the snowy ranges of Cassidy Farm, his exhaustion evaporated as he threw open the door of his silver Dodge Ram and leaped to the ground. His steel-toed boots sank through the buttery soft whiteness and slid a little on the icy layer beneath it.

Yeah, Jade Arletta wasn't driving anywhere in her Jaguar this evening, and he was about to find out why. Jogging across the sidewalk that his twin brothers, Devlin and Emerson, had salted, he let himself in through the double glass entrance doors.

On the other side was one of the biggest indoor farmer's markets in the Texas panhandle. Following a recent expansion and remodel, folks were now driving from all the surrounding counties to purchase their beef, wild honey products, and fresh produce when it was in season. To his left were floor-to-ceiling shelves of preserves, jams, and jerky, along with their signature Cassidy Farm personal indulgence items — candles, soaps, lotions, shampoo, and bath bombs — all crafted from his family's super-secret wild honey recipes. To his right was a coffee bar and bakery.

Claire Cassidy was standing behind one of the glass display cases, chatting merrily and spooning out samples of her latest endeavor, several commercial-sized trays of homemade fudge. His mother's dyed blonde hair was scooped up in a messy bun, and a white apron emblazoned with their company logo was tied around her trim waist — a horse's head with a flowing mane surrounded by a wreath of silver corn stalks.

It was the woman standing on the other side of the counter, however, who captured Beldon's attention and held him riveted in the entryway. An acute sense of awareness crashed through him, like it always did when they were in the same room. It was followed by a bolt of irritation.

Jade Arletta, as it turned out, was not sick or injured like he'd feared. In fact, she'd never looked better. Or less prepared to brave the worsening weather outdoors.

"The peppermint fudge is my favorite, hands down," she gushed as she removed the white plastic sampler spoon from her mouth. The imprint of her hot pink lipstick remained on the tiny neck of the spoon as she discarded it inside the tiny silver trash bucket his mother kept on the cabinet.

Beldon critically eyed the metallic gold sweater sweeping Jade's thighs. Like her black leather pants, it looked more stylish than warm. And her black stiletto boots were a far cry from snow boots. The very thought of her venturing outside dressed like that made him want to toss her over his shoulder and haul her home in his truck. Knowing her, she'd probably accuse him of ruining her designer sweater and use it to blackmail him into doing something he didn't want to do — like manning the kissing booth at the second annual Chipper Hoe Down next fall. The only reason Beldon and his brothers had staffed the first kissing booth was due to her incessant arm-twisting.

It was in that booth that he and Jade had shared an unforgettable second kiss that was now seared into his memory alongside their first kiss.

In what looked like a calculated move, she chose that moment to glance up at the glass case of cakes and pies. Her strawberry blonde hair slid to one side like a silky curtain. She tossed it back, making a set of gold bracelets on her wrist jangle, and their gazes met.

"Oh, hey, Beldon!" she trilled, managing to look surprised, which was laughable. Though he was running a little later than usual, the entire population of Chipper knew his last stop of the day was always at his family's store. The long hours he spent riding the range didn't leave him much time for cooking, so he bought whatever looked good and took it home for dinner. Some evenings it was jalapeño beef jerky. Other evenings it was a sack of his mother's famous hot and spicy sausage kolaches.

Beldon returned Jade's greeting with a rigid nod. The feeling that she was up to something intensified. To avoid a conversation with her, he stalked toward the dry goods shelves, though he would've much preferred to check if there were any kolaches left in the bakery. He nearly bumped into Devlin, who was entering the shop from the Authorized Personnel door leading to the storage room.

In his arms were a stack of crates bearing new wild honey products to be stocked. He was wearing their standard uniform of jeans, cowboy boots, and a button-up shirt bearing their company logo. Unlike the plaid shirts Beldon favored, Devlin preferred solid colors. This evening, he had on an impeccably pressed red shirt, making Beldon feel every speck of the dust and dirt clinging to his own clothing.

"So, ah…" Devlin muttered in undertones as he

stepped around his older brother to drop his load on the checkout counter. He pretended to rearrange the gum and candy display by the cash register. "I kid you not. Jade's been hanging around for the last two hours." He and his twin, Emerson, were the only two brothers who'd inherited their mother's blonde hair. He lifted his hat to run a hand in agitation through the straw-colored strands. "Tried to call and warn you, but you didn't pick up."

Beldon belatedly reached for his phone. Though he kept the ringer turned up, it was nearly impossible to hear it over the whistling winds and baying cattle. Sure enough, he'd missed no less than four calls from Dev.

"What does she want?" he muttered, idly lifting a pack of cinnamon gum from the rack. Though folks liked to come hang out with friends at the coffee bar and bakery, most of them didn't linger for two hours straight — certainly not in the middle of a snowstorm.

"You," his brother informed him bluntly. "Claimed in no uncertain terms that she needed to talk to you directly about something."

Beldon scowled. "I have nothing to say to her."

"Well, you better think of something, because Mom already offered to have you drive her home on account of the weather."

"Why me?" Beldon fixed his brother with an accusing stare, wondering why he hadn't already done the deed.

"Hey, don't kill the messenger." Devlin mockingly held up his hands, eyes twinkling. "I offered, but she seemed bent on waiting for you, and Mom is, well, as oblivious as ever about your intense dislike of this particular neighbor."

Intense dislike? How Beldon felt about Jade was intense alright. He wasn't so sure about the dislike part, though. He should despise her for the way she'd broken Asher's heart a year and a half ago, but he didn't. He couldn't, no matter how hard he tried.

His older brother had finally been able to pick up the pieces and move on, but his ex-girlfriend couldn't take an ounce of credit for it. Asher's recovery was due one hundred percent to Bella Johnson, the new ranch hand who'd blown into their lives last summer. He'd fallen as hard and fast for her as the avalanches currently plaguing the distant canyons. Only a month into their relationship, he'd popped the question. They were planning a June wedding, which was why his brothers were determined to keep Jade as far from the two of them as possible between then and now. She'd done enough damage already. They didn't want to give her any opportunity to ruin Asher's life all over again.

"I'll get her out of here pronto," Beldon growled, snatching up two candy bars and tossing them on the counter. As he dug for his wallet, Dev shook his head and pushed the candy bars back in his direction.

"Mom would shoot me if I charged you for anything."

"Then don't tell her." Beldon peeled off a few dollar bills and tossed them on the counter. Candy bars weren't leftover bakery items that she was going to toss if they didn't sell. He consumed more than his fair share of the leftover donuts and croissants for free, but he had no intention of doing that with their regular inventory.

Stuffing the candy bars in the pocket of his insulated denim jacket, he pivoted toward the coffee shop and found himself face-to-face with the stunning female he'd been volunteered to drive home.

"I hear you need a ride," he informed her brusquely.

Her pine green eyes widened in faux surprise at his tone. "Well, hello to you, too." She held up a white bakery bag, studying him from beneath long, mascara-drenched lashes. The flap was folded down and sealed with a metallic sticker bearing the Cassidy Farm logo. "These are for you. I certainly don't expect you to chauffeur me home for free."

Figuring it was best to ignore her gift, he summoned his steeliest layer of willpower and took a step toward the door. He intended to keep a deadpan expression while he walked around her. However, he caught a whiff of the blasted kolaches, which she must have asked his mom to throw in the toaster oven, and it stopped him dead in his tracks.

He mechanically reached for the bag and kept walking, trying not to think about the way her pink lacquered fingernails grazed his glove. Unfortunately, his stomach gave a rumble of hunger that he was sure she heard. He didn't stop until he reached the front door. Resting a hand on the silver push bar, he waited for her to catch up before opening it.

The wind was wailing louder than when he'd entered the store, and the snow was swirling faster and thicker beneath the hazy purplish glow of sunset. The visibility was worse, too. He could no longer see all the way across the parking lot.

Jade joined him at the door, filling his ears with her sultry alto — a sound he never seemed to get all the way out of his head. "Thank you for accepting my payment. It's the least I could do for putting you to so much trouble on a night like this."

He glanced over at her, wondering why she wasn't buttoning up before heading outside. "Where's your coat?"

"I left it in the car." Her shrug was innocent. "It's probably best to leave it there for now."

He shook his head at the outline of her Jaguar beneath the layer of whiteness, knowing she was right. Even if he knocked off the thickest mounds of snow, the swirling wind would spread the falling crystals all over the expensive leather and chrome interior.

"So help me, Jade," he growled, shrugging out of his own jacket. If the smell of horses and sweat clinging to it offended her snooty sensibilities, it was her own fault for coming inside the store so ill prepared.

"You don't have to do this," she protested as he draped it around her shoulders.

"Tough luck, princess. It's all I've got. If you don't

9

like the smell of horses, that's your problem." He pushed open the door and waved her through it.

"I happen to love the smell of horses, Beldon Cassidy!" Lifting her chin, she stormed past him over the threshold.

The moment her spiky heel hit the snowy sidewalk, however, her boot slid.

"Oh, for crying out loud!" he muttered, reaching for her elbow to steady her. Shoving the bag of kolaches back into her hands, which she had several other shopping bags looped around, he bent to scoop her up in his arms.

She gave a breathy squeal of surprise that didn't sound the least bit fake and clung to him.

Inwardly congratulating himself for putting a dent in her precious composure, he strode with her toward his truck. The wind whipped mercilessly at them, plastering several strands of her hair against the lower half of his face. He caught a whiff of her shampoo. It was a stark reminder of how she refused to use anything on her hair and skin other than Cassidy Farm's wild honey products. She was a spoiled, pampered only child who indulged in the best things her papa's money could buy. The fact that his family's signature line of products made the cut was actually pretty flattering.

Another gust of wind rocked them as they reached the passenger door of his truck. She reached up and clapped a hand over his Stetson to keep it from blowing off.

"Thanks." His voice was gruff as he bent his

knees to open the door of his truck that he'd left unlocked. He dumped her unceremoniously on the passenger side of the seat.

"See? I'm not all bad, cowboy." The simper was back in Jade's voice.

He slammed the door shut before she could say anything else. Jogging around to the driver's door, he yanked it open and climbed behind the wheel, whacking his hat against his boot to remove the snow before tossing it on the dashboard.

"You shouldn't have come out in this weather," he snarled as he started the motor. "It's not safe."

"Aw, I appreciate your concern." Her tone was light and teasing.

"I was referring to your car," he lied.

"It's insured." She sounded close to laughing. "And the only reason I'm out in this weather is because I really need to talk to you."

"We don't have anything to talk about." He shot her an exasperated look and immediately wished he hadn't. She looked good sitting in his truck — too good — like a golden goddess, but with snowflakes melting on her lashes.

"Actually, we do." Her expression sobered. "I just found out that Asher and Bella are thinking of hiring that complete farce of a wedding planner from New York."

"Don't, Jade." He shook his head in warning. He didn't know the first thing about planning a wedding, but that was beside the point. "I told you to stay out of their business, and I meant it." He slowly backed from his parking spot.

"But she's bad news, Beldon. *Really* bad news, I kid you not!"

Talk about the pot calling the kettle black! He turned the truck around and started rolling forward, struggling to keep his temper under control. "How so?" he demanded.

"I have good reason to believe she's going to take their money and skip town."

"And you know this, how?" He didn't know why he bothered asking, since Jade had never been wrong about stuff like this. Long before she'd gotten a pre-law degree under her belt, she could sniff out a liar or a cheat from a mile away.

"The details are in the folder I left under the doormat on your front porch."

He gave her another searching look. "Then why did you come to the store?"

"Because you didn't answer my call from earlier, and you might not have found the folder until it was too late."

"I usually don't hear my phone while I'm out riding." He didn't know why he felt the need to defend himself. Heat crept up the back of his neck at how easy it was for her to get under his skin.

"I am well of aware of that, cowboy. That's why I thought it would be best to grab some face time." Her voice returned to a more cheerful note. "Plus, I needed to run something else past you."

He could hear the crinkle of paper as she unrolled

the bag of kolaches from his family's bakery. The scent of homemade bread and spicy sausage filled the cab.

"Yeah? What's that?" It was impossible to keep his anger churning against her while his mouth was watering like Niagara Falls.

"I could do it, Beldon." Her voice came out in a rush. "I know what you're probably thinking, but just hear me out."

Alarm bells jangled in his mind. "You could do what?" he asked carefully, not taking his eyes off the road. It was slow going in the thick snow. They hadn't yet made it off the long gravel driveway leading to the main road. The snow was so thick now that he could barely feel the bump of the chains around his tires. The trip from Cassidy Ranch to her childhood home should've taken less than two minutes. In this weather, it was probably going to take at least ten times longer.

"I could help them plan the wedding. It wouldn't cost them a penny. Promise! Y'all are like family, so it would be my gift."

"What?" He shot her an incredulous look, unable to believe she was even suggesting something as preposterous as helping plan her ex's wedding. "Absolutely no—!" The rest of the word was abruptly silenced when she stuffed a sausage-filled kolache into his mouth.

He lightly gripped it with his teeth, swallowing a snort of laughter at her audacity. *You little buzzard!* "Jade," he warned in a voice muffled by the kolache.

"Did you say something?" she asked sweetly. "Sorry, but it's a little hard to understand you right now."

"Yes," he growled, but even he couldn't make out what he was saying.

"Here, I'll help." She impishly reached over to remove the last half of the kolache and popped the end of it into her own mouth. "Oh, my land, but your mama can cook!" she sighed.

She and his brothers had been sharing beverages and digging into the same popcorn bowls their entire lives, but this felt different. They were all grown up now, making the gesture feel more intimate. More like flirting.

He chewed and swallowed past the lump in his throat, wishing he and Jade could go back to the days before they'd become enemies. "My answer is still no about planning the wedding."

"Why not?" She shrugged out of his jacket, leaving it draped on the seat cushion between them. She lifted another kolache to his mouth. "You know I could do it. I know this town like the back of my hand, along with every venue and vendor in it."

"That's not the point." He dipped his head greedily to take the sausage and bread into his mouth. The pads of her fingers brushed the side of his mouth in the process, sending a shot of warmth straight to his heart. A stab of remorse followed at the realization he had absolutely no right to enjoy her touch. She was his oldest brother's ex-girlfriend, which made her off limits to him. He and his five brothers had agreed back in high school never to date each other's exes.

"Asher and I smoothed things over months ago. What's in the past is in the past." Her voice gentled, as if she was trying to soothe a prickly kitten.

He couldn't believe she was pushing so hard for something so unreasonable. "I agree, and he's moved on. You need to do the same." Asher's wedding was off limits to her. Period. The sooner she got that through her beautiful, stubborn head, the better for them all.

"Oh, my lands, Beldon! You're impossible!" she seethed, finally dropping her pretense at sugary sweetness. "I don't know why I even bothered coming to you about this."

He snorted. "Maybe because you knew it was pointless to go around me?" He'd been watchdogging Asher's back day and night ever since the kissing booth fiasco last summer. She was up to something. He could practically hear the wheels spinning inside her conniving brain.

"No, you hard-nosed cowpoke. I was actually foolish enough to think you would listen. In the past, you were the voice of reason among your brothers and our circle of friends."

Yeah, well, that ship had sailed when she'd broken up with Asher, which incidentally was the same day he'd exited the hospital with a face full of burn scars. Her timing couldn't have been worse.

"Friends are people you can trust," he reminded stiffly. "Man, but it's as hot as a thousand blazes in here," he grumbled beneath his breath. He hadn't meant to admit out loud how badly she was getting under his skin, but he was sweating bullets. A swift glance at the thermostat revealed why. It was jacked up to nearly ninety degrees, something he never would have done on purpose. Either he'd bumped it on accident, or the woman sitting beside him had nudged it up when he wasn't looking.

He shot her a suspicious look.

Her answering snicker verified that she was, indeed, the culprit.

Glaring, he mashed the button to roll down his window, *all* the way down. A blast of cold air and snow swirled into the cab. *Paybacks are tough, princess!* He thoroughly enjoyed the shiver that worked its way through her shoulders and on down the rest of her slender frame.

Still giggling, she retrieved the coat she'd tossed over the back of the seat. "I'm surprised you even noticed, given how thick your skull is."

"This isn't about us, Jade."

"Really?" Her smile vanished. "Because it kind of feels like it is."

"It's not."

"So you're *not* continuing to stonewall everything I do to punish me for what happened the day before the fire?"

She was referring to their ill-timed first kiss, of course. He could still remember every detail of what had led up to it like it was yesterday. She'd been freaking out about how she and Asher had been steadily growing apart and almost rammed her car into his truck. In the process of trying to figure out if she was injured, they'd ended up in each other's arms on the side of the road. What happened next shouldn't have.

"I didn't plan on kissing you that day," she informed him shakily. "You know I didn't. I was upset and not thinking clearly." Her words were followed by a violent shiver.

"I know." He rolled up the window, well aware that he bore as much guilt over it as she did, since he'd sure as heck kissed her back. He'd probably never know the full extent of the damage their necking had done to her already flailing relationship with his brother. It couldn't have helped, though. To this day, he felt responsible for their breakup and the mountain of heartache that followed.

"Then why won't you forgive me and let it go?"

"I think you know why." The truth was, he'd long since forgiven her. Letting the matter go, however, was proving to be a bigger problem. He still had feelings for her. That's why he had to keep his distance.

"Right. Because of you and your brothers' stupid rule," she conceded in a dull voice. "I can't believe you guys are still hanging on to something so juvenile. We're not in high school anymore."

"Maybe not, but we're still brothers. When you hurt one of us, you hurt us all."

"I've apologized to every one of your brothers," she said wearily. "Your parents, too. I don't know what else you want from me."

"Nothing, Jade. I know it bothers you that Asher has found real happiness with someone else, but it's time to let it go. I won't stand by and do nothing while you spoil things for him again."

A stony silence settled between them as he nosed his truck onto the snowy highway and drove the short distance to the ranch adjacent to Cassidy Farm.

When a faint sniffle met his ears, his heart sank. "Listen, I didn't mean to make you cry." The sound of her misery made him feel like a monster. He'd grown up next door to her. Once upon a time, they'd been friends. Not as close as she'd ever been with Asher, but good friends all the same.

"You didn't," she snapped. "I'm battling a cold."

He knew she was lying, which only made him feel worse. As he rolled up the driveway at a snail's pace, he searched for something to say that would restore peace between them. Before he could come up with anything halfway intelligent, a white van materialized in the glow of the solar lights lining the driveway.

Beldon edged his truck as far to the right as he could without sliding into the ditch. The two vehicles passed each other with only inches to spare. He was so close to the van that there was no way to miss the lettering on the magnetic sign affixed to its rear panel. *West Texas Home Health Services.* Unless he was mistaken, it was a company that provided personalized nursing visits.

Beldon's head swiveled in Jade's direction. "Is

everything okay with your parents?" he asked quickly.

She gave him a withering look. "Of course. Why wouldn't it be?"

"Eh, maybe because a home health services van just exited the property?"

"Maybe they made a wrong turn." She shrugged. "Not sure why you care. You just finished making it pretty clear that we aren't friends anymore."

"I said no such thing, and of course I care about you and your family," he shot back in exasperation. The problem was that he cared too much! More than he had any right to.

She ignored his outburst. "You also made it brutally clear that I'm supposed to stay out of your family's business, so you need to stay out of ours in return. That's how this works."

He braked in the circle drive at the steps of her veranda. The enormous three-story ranch was ablaze with lights. A shadowy figure waited on the other side of a pair of glass scrollwork doors.

"Jade." He swiveled in her direction, seeking answers. "We're still neighbors. If your family ever needs anything from my family—"

"We don't," she informed him flatly, shrugging out of his coat and tossing it on the seat cushion between them. "But if you care half as much for Asher as you claim you do, you'll show him the contents of the folder I left on your front porch."

"I will." As he reached for his door handle, she

shook her head fiercely, looking so close to bursting into tears that he grew still.

"Don't bother," she said coldly. "I'd rather crawl to my front door than force you to spend one second longer in my evil presence."

He could hear the hurt in her voice and feared he'd finally pushed her too far. Even so, he'd been raised to be a gentleman. There was no way he was sitting on his duff while she risked her neck on the icy porch steps in her ridiculously high heels.

His weariness from earlier returned as he pushed open his door and leaped to the ground.

Jade's eyes shot green sparks at him as he hurried to her side, but she didn't put up any resistance when he cupped a hand beneath her elbow. He guided her up the steps and paused with her in front of the double doors.

"You can go now." She reached for the door handle on the right.

"I meant what I said, Jade. If your family ever needs anything..." He let the words rest between them.

"I'll send a tow truck for my car in the morning."

He hated leaving things like this between them. "Jade, please."

"This is goodbye, Beldon." She wrenched open the front door and stepped inside.

He caught a brief glimpse of Tandy Arletta tipping her face up from a chair to receive a kiss on the forehead from her daughter. Like his mother, she normally sported perfect hair and makeup. This evening, however, Tandy's hair was wrapped in a bright-colored turban. A quilt covered her legs. Beldon's sense that something was wrong increased.

Come to think of it, the entry foyer was an odd place for her to be sitting and waiting for her daughter. Had she been that worried about Jade being caught out in the snowstorm?

He returned to his truck, knowing the only thing he could do for Jade this evening was rescue her Jaguar from the pile of snow it would soon be buried in. Before driving away from her home, he pulled out his cell phone and texted an SOS to his brothers. They quickly came up with a plan to meet in the store parking lot with shovels to dig out her car and a trailer to transport it to one of their barns for the night.

He sniffed the air curiously as he revved the motor. It smelled like his mother's workshop when she was whipping up a new batch of wild honey lotion. His gaze landed on the floorboard where Jade had left one of her shopping bags.

Leaning over to reach for the paper handles, he was amazed when the whole top of the bag lifted from the floor. Flipping on his cab light, he discovered that the bottom half remained sticking to the floor mat, because one of the bottles had busted.

It was strange since a member of his family personally checked the seal on each one. A closer glance revealed that the bottle hadn't busted, after all. It had been unscrewed and left open, lying on its side — probably to ensure that his truck would smell exactly the way it was smelling right now.

Beldon's lips twitched. Apparently, Jade's sense of humor was still very much intact. He'd hurt her feelings, but he hadn't broken her spirit.

The drive back to Cassidy Farm turned into twenty minutes of sheer torture, since his truck cab was enveloped in her favorite scent. He could think of nothing besides Jade, her sass, and her kisses that had brought him to the edge of insanity — not once, but twice.

"You're killing me, woman," he muttered as he pulled into the store parking lot. "Absolutely killing me."

If his brothers got a whiff of his truck cab, they would have questions he wasn't in the mood to answer, which was probably Jade's plan all along. Yep, she could hold her own when it came to paybacks.

CHAPTER 2: EX ENCOUNTER

JADE

OF COURSE *I care about you and your family!*

Beldon's words continued to ring like music in Jade's ears. Throughout the next several weeks, she played them again and again inside her head. They were enough to snap her out of her melancholy so she could get back to work. He could warn her away from his oldest brother all he wanted, but he couldn't turn off his feelings for her any more than she could turn off her feelings for him. His problem was that he was so tied up in knots by his own honor that it was choking him to death.

At the moment, there was nothing she could do about his stubbornness, though. She was too busy trying to save Asher and Bella from their upcoming wedding disaster. It was the middle of April, only two short months away from their big day, and they didn't so much as have a cake on order. Jade knew this because she was personally acquainted with every bakery owner between Chipper and Amarillo.

Thankfully, Asher and Beldon had sent the scam artist wedding planner running for the hills, but Bella was still floundering. From what Jade could gather, the former school-teacher-turned-ranch-hand didn't own a wedding dress, have a venue reserved, flowers picked out, or musicians lined up. And absolutely no one Jade knew had yet to receive a formal invitation in the mail. At the rate things were going, there might not even *be* a wedding if someone didn't step up to the plate soon and take charge.

Bella needs my help. With every passing day, Jade became more and more convinced of that fact. Despite Beldon's warning for her to keep her nose solidly out of the wedding preparations, she was actually starting to feel guilty for doing so.

The only thing that had given her a break from the guilt was her current job search. As her mother's condition grew worse, her father was spending more time at her bedside, which meant his regular chores around the ranch weren't getting done. In short, money was growing tight.

So Jade had done something about it. And just this morning, her job search had culminated in a life-changing decision. The fact that she was now a junior partner in a law firm was still sinking in as she stepped out of Buck Harrington's red brick office. It was located in the tiny but growing downtown area of Chipper. On her way to the car she'd left parked at the curb, she glanced idly around her. Her gaze landed on the love of Asher Cassidy's life.

Bella Johnson was sitting alone at a sidewalk cafe.

A yellow umbrella was stretched open above her table, but she didn't seem to be enjoying the cheerful scene. Her head was down, and she was twirling a straw around and around in her glass. There was a decidedly dejected air about her movements. Her dark hair was pulled back in a French braid, and she was slowly swinging her crossed jean-clad legs.

Jade wished she was wearing something more casual than her red silk suit and navy stilettos. However, she wasn't the kind of woman to let an opportunity like this go to waste. Since Beldon Cassidy wasn't here to stop her, she squared her shoulders and fluttered her hand in a wave.

"Hey, Bella!"

Bella's legs stopped swinging. Her whole body tensed as she raised tormented blue-gray eyes to meet Jade's gaze. They were red-rimmed from weeping.

The last of Jade's reservations about approaching the woman fled. She was a take-action kind of gal, and right now Bella Johnson was in desperate need of…something. Comfort, maybe? All Jade knew was that she wouldn't have ignored a perfect stranger who looked this miserable, so she wasn't about to walk past the fiancée of a man she'd adored her entire life.

She click-clacked the short distance down the sidewalk to stand beside the table with the yellow umbrella. "Are you okay?"

Bella's heart-shaped face crumpled in misery. "Do I look okay? Seriously, Jade, if you came to gloat about how badly I'm in over my head with this wedding stuff—"

"No!" Jade interrupted quickly. "That's not who I am." Drawing a deep breath, she plunged onward. "I know we got off to a bad start, which was entirely my fault, so I, ah...I'm sorry. For all of it."

Bella's mouth twisted. "Yeah. It was a pretty rough first encounter." She'd been so nervous that she'd knocked over a glass of tea, spilling it down the front of Jade's silk blouse. "It wasn't entirely your fault, though. I'm the one who spilled the tea and ruined your shirt."

Rolling her eyes, Jade hastened to assure her. "I couldn't have cared less about my shirt. I was just trying to strong-arm the Cassidy brothers into manning the kissing booth at the hoedown, and you handed me the perfect ammunition. I'm sorry you got caught in the crossfire."

"You're kidding!" Bella searched her gaze. Then a snicker escaped her. "Are you telling me you were only pretending to be angry about your shirt?"

"Yep, and I really am sorry about the way I treated you that day. To be honest, I was barely keeping it together with the way Asher kept snapping and growling after everything I said. Not to mention the way his brothers were staring daggers at me."

Bella's smile widened. "They're like a pack of wolves when they're riled, aren't they?"

"Couldn't have said it better myself!"

As the familiar ache of their rejection radiated

through Jade, Bella waved impulsively at the three empty chairs around the table. "Feel free to join me."

"I would love to. Thanks." Jade dumped her purse and briefcase in the closest chair and took a seat in the one across from Bella. "Gosh, I can't tell you how good it feels to take a load off! My limit for walking in four-inch heels is a flat two hours. Not a second longer."

Looking fascinated, Bella leaned her elbows on the table and dropped her chin into her hands. "Then why do you wear them?"

"Because I love how they look." More importantly, Jade loved how they made everyone else look, especially Beldon Cassidy. He tended to hover over her when she was wearing heels, as if he was afraid she might break her neck without his hawk-eyed assistance.

"You're much braver than me." Bella shook her head. "I'm such a klutz that I can barely walk in boots and sneakers. Sometimes I trip for no reason at all."

Jade smiled sympathetically. "It's probably because you're more tired than you realize. You have a lot on your plate right now."

Her words brought a prickle of tears to Bella's eyes.

"I'm sorry." Jade reached in consternation across the table. "I wasn't trying to make you feel inadequate."

"It's alright." Bella blinked rapidly and brushed

at the dampness gathering in the corners of her eyes. "I'm just having a bad day."

"Is there anything I can do to help?" Jade signaled the waiter, sensing that the conversation might take a while. The negotiating she'd done for the past two hours next door had left her mouth as dry as cotton balls.

"No, but thanks for asking." Bella lowered her elbows from the table and resumed her aimless straw stirring. "Today is the anniversary of my gram's passing. She was my last living relative. Add that to the wedding looming on the horizon, and it's been an all-around miserable day."

Jade's sympathies escalated. With no sisters of her own, plus a wheelchair-bound mother to boot, she was all too familiar with the feeling of being alone in the world.

The waiter approached, and Jade placed an order for a glass of peach tea. "Listen, I heard that things fell through with your wedding planner."

"Oh, really?" Bella's expression brightened with amusement. "Considering that you're the person who submitted a legal treatise to Beldon with seventeen pages of reasons against hiring her…"

"Oh." Jade dropped her gaze, swallowing a laugh. "You heard about that."

"I did. Thanks, by the way."

Jade eagerly raised her gaze once again. "You're not mad about my interference?"

"No way! I'm grateful." Bella's voice was sincere. "I lost my entire life savings to my ex, so I can't afford to lose what little I've managed to accumulate since then — certainly not two months before our wedding. Otherwise, I'll be wearing these jeans and boots when I walk down the aisle."

"Heaven forbid!" Jade shuddered. That certainly explained why Bella hadn't ordered a cake or flowers yet. "If you don't mind me asking, what did your ex do with your money?"

With a self-recriminatory groan, Bella dropped her face into her hands. "We bought a house together after we got engaged." When she raised her head again, her cheeks were flaming with embarrassment. "His apartment lease came due, and we agreed it was best for him to move in early. Stupid, I know, since possession is nine-tenths of the law." She lowered her hands to her lap. "Shortly afterward, I found out he was cheating on me, and ugh! I really don't want to talk about this anymore."

"Just one more question," Jade pressed. The lawyer in her couldn't resist slogging through the details. "Did both of you sign the contract to purchase your home?"

"I did, and I realize it means he owes me my share of the down payment. That said…" She let out a long-suffering sigh.

"I take it, he's refusing to pay it back."

"Yes. Sort of." Bella waved a hand tiredly. "He claims he's not ready to sell the house because he still wants to patch things up between us."

"Sounds like a load of bull to me."

"Pretty much. Asher has his family attorney

looking into it, but I'm not getting my hopes up. I know legal stuff takes time, and who knows if it'll even be worth it in the end?" She shook her head. "With my luck, it'll take so long to get the guy to fork over my money that I'll end up owing more in legal fees than the size of my settlement."

"Maybe not." Jade accepted her glass of peach tea from the waiter and took a sip.

Bella knit her eyebrows together. "What do you mean?"

Jade smiled over the rim of her glass, knowing she was about to reveal something that few people besides her parents knew. "I have a law degree, so I know what I'm talking about."

Bella's expression remained glum. "Yeah, Asher mentioned something about you studying pre-law."

"I did." Jade waved a hand impatiently. "Then I went on and finished my graduate level coursework and sat for the bar exam."

"Meaning you're an honest-to-gosh lawyer?" Bella sat back in her chair, looking stunned.

"I'm a lawyer," Jade affirmed. "A non-practicing one until this morning, though. I've done a little charity work here and there to keep my license active, but that's about to change." She pointed at the law office next door. "Buck Harrington wants to retire, and he doesn't think his son is ready to run the practice alone. Long story short, they're bringing me onboard as a junior partner."

"Congratulations!" Bella stared at her a moment. "Wow!"

"Thanks!" Jade raised her tea glass. "To better days ahead for both of us."

"To better days ahead." Bella clinked her tea glass against Jade's and took a sip. "I'm not sure when those better days are going to show up, but I like your optimism."

"I wasn't just blowing smoke in your face." Jade set down her glass and considered her next words carefully, knowing she was about to interfere big time in Bella's business. "If you let me have a run at your ex, I can have that settlement in your hands before the end of the week."

Bella choked on her sip of tea. She tapped a fist to her chest as she set down her glass, coughing. "Again, I like your optimism, but I can't afford two lawyers. I'm not sure I can even afford one."

"I wasn't planning on charging you." Jade warmed to the topic, thrilled that Bella hadn't shot down her offer before she had the chance to explain. "It'll be my wedding gift to you and Asher. All I need is that joker's name and the address of the home you bought together."

Bella caught her lower lip between her teeth, and a long drag of silence settled between them. It ended when she jerked forward to rest her clenched hands on the table. "I can't believe I'm agreeing to this, but I'm desperate. His name is Jim Steering. He's a high school principal in Dallas." She rattled off his street address. "Just watch your step with him. Whatever he put in my teacher file has pretty much rendered me un-hireable in any school district. I wouldn't want him doing the same to your career."

Though Jade kept a smile on her face, her temper flared beneath the surface. *Oh, honey! He's not going to know what even hit him after I'm through with him.* She'd run into plenty of bullies like Jim Steering, and she knew exactly what strings to tug in order to make them squawk like babies. A job like his made him particularly vulnerable, since he couldn't afford any bad press.

She glanced at her watch. It was a few minutes shy of noon, which meant there was plenty of time left for her to catch an evening flight out of Amarillo. Or she could skip the airport and just drive the six hours or so from Chipper to Dallas.

"When I get back into town with your check," she leaned forward in her seat to pin Bella with a questioning look, "you can additionally count on me to help out with whatever else you need. Addressing invitations, sampling cakes, providing moral support during dress fittings, the whole enchilada."

Bella, who had taken another sip of her iced tea, seemed to be having trouble swallowing. She finally regained her voice. "Like a wedding planner?"

"Why not? Nearly everyone else in town considers me their go-to gal when it comes to event planning. I already have the perfect Rolodex of vendors. Plus, a lot of people owe me favors," she bragged.

"I accept." Bella looked a little dazed. "My only request is that you keep your involvement on the down-low for the sake of the Cassidys, at least for now."

"Deal." Jade had already planned to do exactly that. She raised her tea glass at Bella. She did the same, and they clinked them together again.

Bella twisted the tail of one dark braid around her finger. "I don't know how to thank you. I'm so out of my league with this wedding stuff that it's laughable."

"Don't worry. We'll have this event organized in two snaps." Jade was confident in her abilities when it came to stuff like that.

"I reckon the next step is getting Asher's thumbs up on your offer," Bella mused.

"If he says no, I'll step out of the picture." Jade gave a decided nod. "Even from a distance, though, I can wrangle discounts on the cake and flowers for you."

Worry scrunched Bella's forehead. "Why are you helping me?" she asked suddenly. "For real."

Jade didn't have to ponder her answer. "Because I love the Cassidys, despite everything that's happened." If that sounded sappy, then so be it. It was the truth. "I'm sorry I hurt Asher over the way I broke up with him, but I still care for him and his family. I always will." She hoped Bella wouldn't read the wrong thing into her words. The romance was over between her and Asher, but she was never going to hate him, and she was never going to stop fighting to restore their friendship.

Bella shifted uncomfortably in her seat. "For a

while there last summer, I was afraid you were trying to break us up. That you wanted him back."

"No." Jade shook her head. "Though I will always care for Asher and his family, we weren't right for each other. I know that now, and so does he." She stared into the distance, trying to put her thoughts into words. "It was fun dating him, don't get me wrong, but we were never in love. If we'd gone on and tied the knot the way folks expected us to, we would have both lived to regret it."

Something that Jade couldn't define wafted across Bella's fine-boned features. "How did you know you weren't in love with Asher?" While the question hung between them, she flushed. "I know that sounds like a dumb question, but I thought I was in love with Jim Steering — right up to the point that I caught him cheating on me."

"I thought I was in love for a while, too." Jade ran a finger down the moisture beading against the side of her glass. "I had no idea what I was missing until I finally fell in love. For real this time." There were days she wished she'd never made the discovery because of all the pain it had brought her and those she cared for.

Bella's eyes narrowed in speculation. "I didn't realize you were dating anyone."

"I'm not." Jade's mouth flat-lined. "As it turns out, the guy I fell for isn't interested in dating me."

"No way!" Bella's mouth fell open.

Her astonishment was a soothing balm to Jade's damaged pride. "It's nice of you to say that."

"This isn't about being nice." Bella's blue-gray eyes snapped with interest. "This is my way of saying that I know about the Cassidy brothers' infamous Rule."

"Oh." Jade felt the air seep out of her. She'd not been expecting Bella to connect the dots with how little she'd disclosed about her dismal love life.

"I'm not supposed to know about it, but I do." Bella snorted in exasperation. "Let's just say that Fox was pretty loose-lipped with me last summer while he was recovering from his concussion."

"That sounds like Fox." Jade had tried to visit him in the hospital after his bronc riding accident, but he'd refused to see her. He was insanely loyal to his brothers, and his loyalty meant he was keeping his distance from her.

"So, which brother did you fall for?" Bella wheedled. "I know it's none of my business, but I'm sort of dying to know now that you brought it up."

Jade's eye widened. "You have to ask? I figured it would be obvious to an insider like you."

"Hmm." A secretive smile crept across Bella's features as she drummed her fingers against the table. "Fox is too much of a moron for a woman with your class, Devlin and Emerson are too nerdy, and Asher is taken. So that leaves Beldon and Cormac. Holy guacamole!" Her eyes widened as the truth sank in. "You're right. It's pretty obvious when you think about it."

Jade spread her hands helplessly. "It doesn't

matter. He's never going to date his brother's left-overs. He's made that painfully clear."

Bella studied her in sympathy. "Knowing Beldon, if he cares for you as much as you care for him, he's never going to date anyone else, either. He is seriously the most noble guy I've ever met."

"That he is." Jade blinked away the haze of moisture forming over her eyes. "He takes it to ridiculous levels."

"But it's more than that, isn't it?" Bella's gaze grew troubled. "The Cassidys are grown men. There's no way the situation between you and Beldon is simply about their silly rule."

"Fine. It's more, but that's something Beldon will have to work out with Asher when he's ready."

"Oh, sheesh! You fell for each other *before* the big break-up, huh?"

"Something like that."

"Before or after the fire?"

"Before." It was a relief for Jade to finally share her woes with another human being. "It's why I *had* to break-up. It was the only right thing to do, under the circumstances."

Bella nodded. "I agree, but Beldon must have felt responsible for your break-up."

"He does, which is completely crazy, because it happened while I was freaking out over the fact that things were already over between Asher and me. It was just a matter of who would break up first. I was so upset about it that I nearly had a head-on collision with Beldon on the highway. He dragged me out of my car to check for injuries, and one thing led to another."

"Oh, snap! You kissed," Bella breathed in awe.

"We kissed." The memory of their first kiss was still potent enough to take Jade's breath away.

"And now you're in love with him."

"Yes." It was the first time Jade had ever admitted it out loud to anyone, even herself. She closed her eyes, allowing the pain of Beldon's rejection to wash over her all over again.

Something soft was pressed into her hand. Jade's eyelids fluttered open to stare at the white tissue. *Oh, sheesh! I'm crying.* Dabbing it at her cheeks, she gave Bella a watery smile. "Guess you weren't the only one feeling a little overwhelmed this morning. I'm in love with a man I can't have, I have a new job I haven't told anyone about yet, and my mother was recently diagnosed with—"

Ugh! She hadn't planned to mention her mother. It just sort of slipped out while she was wailing about the rest of her problems. A tear trickled down her cheek. She wryly wiped it away. Since her final interview with the Harringtons was behind her, it no longer mattered if her makeup was perfect.

"I'm so sorry about your mother!" Bella reached out to touch Jade's hand. "If you ever want to talk about it, I'm a good listener. Nothing you say will get past me."

Jade sniffled. "We barely know each other. I shouldn't unload on you like this."

"Oh, for crying out loud!" Bella exploded. "It's a

small town with few women in it. What few of us there are need to stick together."

Jade studied her wearily as she debated how much to tell her. "Eh, why not? It's Multiple Sclerosis," she admitted. "My mom is in a wheelchair that she'll probably never come out of. She's refusing to leave the house, claiming she doesn't want her friends to see her like this." She drew a bracing breath. "She's been sick for a while. We just didn't know what it was until recently. That's the real reason I'm still living with my parents instead of getting a place of my own. They spoiled me rotten growing up. Now it's my turn to take care of them."

"Family always comes first." Bella's features were tight with conviction. "I lived with Gram until the day she died, and I have no regrets."

"You're right." Jade nodded tearfully. "Guess that means I should quit worrying about the way things are so messed up between Beldon and me. It's not like I have time for a relationship right now." With as fast as her mother's condition was progressing, she wanted to spend every spare minute with her that they had left.

"Beldon would understand." Bella sounded one hundred percent convinced.

Jade wasn't so sure. "Really? Because he made it pretty clear a few weeks ago that we're not even friends anymore." She didn't bother hiding her bitter tone. Now that Bella knew her story, she was the one person in the world Jade didn't have to keep pretending around.

"I don't believe that for one second!" Bella exclaimed.

"That's what he said," Jade fiddled with her tea glass, "in so many words." It had hurt then, and it was still hurting now. She couldn't bear the thought of losing Beldon for good — nice, quiet, peaceful Beldon. He was the rock of the Cassidy brothers.

"I hear you, but sometimes people say things in the heat of the moment that they don't really mean."

"He didn't stutter," Jade pointed out dully.

Bella pursed her lips. "I don't think he's ever been in love before. That's enough to put anyone in a lather, even Beldon. Gosh! Especially Beldon. Can you imagine?" She chuckled. "He's normally so level-headed and in control, and now he's in love and no longer completely in control of his feelings."

Jade knew Bella was trying to be nice, but she knew better than to get her hopes up. "I honestly have no idea if he feels the same way about me as I do about him." Yeah, she'd gotten a reaction out of him with a couple of kisses, but that didn't mean he was in love with her.

"Of course he does!" Bella rolled her eyes. "He wouldn't be knee-jerking the whole situation so badly if he didn't."

Jade tried to take comfort in her words. "For what it's worth, thank you for saying that." She glanced at her watch again and pushed away her half-empty tea glass. "I should go if I'm going to catch a flight to Dallas."

"You mean today?" Bella looked taken aback.

Jade scooted her chair back from the table. "I can't think of a better time. Your wedding is only two months away, and I don't start my new job until next week."

"Okay, then. Today," Bella repeated faintly.

"More likely tomorrow," Jade corrected, "by the time I catch a flight and make it there." She grinned. "But, yes. I'm heading straight to the airport from here. I keep an overnight bag in my car for last-minute changes of plans like this. I've never been one to sit around and wait for things to happen."

"Except when it comes to Beldon," Bella pointed out softly.

"Ouch!" Jade wagged a finger at her. "The kind-hearted school teacher unleashes her claws at long last."

"I was just pointing out something you might not be able to see since you're too close to the situation."

"I can see it." Jade lowered her hand. "For the life of me, though, I have no idea what to do about it. Beldon is too rock solid in his convictions to be bought, swindled, or swayed. It's one of the reasons I love him so much."

"Boy, you have it bad for the guy!" Bella stood and faced her.

"I'll deny it if you tell anyone else."

"Who would I tell?" Bella rolled her shoulders as if working out a cramp.

"Asher, maybe?"

"If you keep my confidences, I'll keep yours. That's how friendship works." Bella held out a hand.

Jade stared at it in surprise. "You seriously want to be my friend?"

"I didn't an hour ago, but hearing your side of the story changed my mind." Bella kept her hand outstretched. "You're a good person, Jade. Better than I ever gave you credit for."

"Oh, come on! Did you not just sit there and listen to my tearful confession about the bazillions of mistakes I've made?"

"Everybody makes mistakes. If I was holding out for perfection, I wouldn't have any friends at all. Besides, I have this sneaking suspicion that you and I are going to be family someday."

Jade longed to believe her. As an attorney, however, she wasn't accustomed to taking leaps of faith. She never moved forward with a case until she had irrefutable evidence in hand. And right now, the facts were not pointing toward a happily-ever-after for her and Beldon.

Still, it would be nice to have a friend again. The town as a whole had given her the cold shoulder after she'd broken things off with Asher. The past year had been the toughest, loneliest year of her life.

Before she could talk herself out of it, she shook Bella's hand.

CHAPTER 3:
REVELATIONS

BELDON

BELDON STEPPED out of the bank, whistling. It had been a record month for the cattle side of the business at Cassidy Farm. So much so that his parents had insisted on giving him a bonus. Though his home construction was complete, he'd been saving money, so he could properly deck out the place. He didn't believe in going into debt, so most of the rooms in his home were currently empty of furniture. The bonus he'd just deposited, however, meant he could now afford to do anything he wanted with the place.

The problem was, he had no idea what he wanted. Back in his teens, he'd imagined he would be married by the time he was pushing thirty. However, his twenty-ninth birthday was approaching, and he didn't have a girlfriend yet. He didn't even have any prospects.

Though Jade's classical features wafted across his mind, he forced himself to stop thinking about her as he strode to the parking lot. He rarely parked by the entrance doors of the stacked stone bank building, because most of the parking spots up close weren't big enough for his full-sized pickup with its extended side-view mirrors. He preferred the far end of the lot, where he could take two parking spots without feeling guilty.

It also gave him a clear view of Main Street, a road that seemed to become busier with every trip he made into town. The newly elected mayor had even installed parking meters and painted parallel parking stripes on both sides of the road. Most of the old-timers refused to use them, claiming it was ridiculous for a town as small as theirs to charge for parking. However, the younger generation liked the option of dropping a few quarters into a slot and being able to park directly in front of the building they were heading inside.

As he swung open his truck door and prepared to leap behind the steering wheel, a flash of green paint caught his eye a few buildings down. There was only one car in town that exact shade of emerald. Stepping away from his truck so he could see around an electric pole, he found himself staring at none other than Jade Arletta's Jaguar. It was parked in front of Buck Harrington's law office, of all places.

A peal of female laughter at the cafe next door to the bank made his shoulders tense. He recognized the voice all too well. It was followed by a second peal of laughter from another female voice that he recognized.

Shading his eyes, he found Jade and Bella chatting at a patio table with a yellow umbrella. As usual, Jade was using her hands to talk. At one point, Bella leaned closer to peer past Jade's shoulder at something on Jade's cell phone. Whatever they were viewing together on the screen made them laugh again.

Beldon scowled, wondering when the two of them had become friends. Never in his wildest imagination would he have pegged his oldest brother's ex-girlfriend and current fiancée as candidates for friendship. Apparently, he'd been wrong.

It was unsettling to witness them getting along, especially after he'd specifically requested that Jade stay away from both Bella and Asher. He couldn't fathom what they had to talk about, unless...

Anger churned in him at the possibility that Jade had utterly ignored his warning about the wedding ceremony and was right now butting into his oldest brother's business. Again. Though unconscionable, it would be just like her. She probably couldn't stand the thought of any event taking place in their small town that she wasn't personally in charge of.

While he debated whether he should approach the two women, the front door of Buck Harrington's law office opened, and Buck's son stepped out. Richard Harrington was a chip off the old block. He wore the same nauseating designer suits and the same slicked back hair style as his father. During the winter when they had their black trench coats on, they could easily pass for mafia members.

Like Beldon, Richard must have overheard Jade and Bella's laughter, because he made a beeline for them. Jade glanced up, smiling brightly as the natty young lawyer swaggered their way. She didn't pull away when he slid an arm around her shoulders and leaned in to air-kiss her cheek.

Jade's body language when she pivoted to introduce him to Bella was one of openness and excitement.

Bella clapped before extending her hand to Richard.

He shook it heartily and appeared to be in no hurry to get moving. In the end, Bella was the first to wave goodbye. She walked away, leaving Jade alone with Richard.

Not wanting to witness any more of their canoodling, Beldon turned away and swung into the cab of his truck. He started the ignition, trying not to care that Jade had finally moved on from Asher. *And me.* He hadn't caught wind of any gossip about her and Richard yet, so their relationship must be new.

Not that it was any of his business, but she could've done so much better than that prepster. Sure, Richard was a lawyer and could afford to indulge her expensive tastes in, well, everything. As a cowboy, though, he was sorely lacking. The guy was better versed in hair products than livestock, and he had so much starch ironed into his shirts that he probably couldn't pick up a pen if he dropped it on the ground.

The mere thought of him getting romantic with

Jade made Beldon's blood boil. He knew he had no right to feel that way, but he was stupidly jealous of the creep. He hunched his shoulders over the steering wheel, trying to get a grip before he started driving.

What have you done to me, Jade? Ever since their last kiss, his insides had been twisted in knots. His oldest brother had slapped down the money for it at the kissing booth during Chipper's First Annual Hoedown. It was supposed to be a joke — payback for Jade strong-arming the Cassidy brothers into manning the booth. However, there'd been nothing funny about the way Jade's lips had moved against his. His response to it had been no laughing matter, either.

By now, he was beyond trying to convince himself that his feelings for her weren't real. Not only were they real, but he was pretty sure they weren't going away anytime soon. Probably never. But that wasn't even his biggest problem. The Rule he and his brothers had made back in high school about not dating each other's exes wasn't his biggest problem, either, though it was kind of cute that Jade had gotten so worked up about it.

The real problem was that he'd been crushing on her for a very long time — not just since their first kiss or their second kiss, but for years. For as long as he could remember, he'd loved her. In return, she'd spent most of that time acting barely aware of his existence.

She and Fox had always traded insults. She and

the twins had once collaborated on a science project. She and Cormac endlessly debated farming techniques, and she and Asher had dated for so long that the town had jokingly merged their names to Jader. Beldon was the only Cassidy brother she'd never spent much time with. They had nothing in common. No shared hobbies or interests.

Unless you count kissing. Beldon's heart pounded every time he thought about the two kisses they'd shared. Yep. Kissing was the one thing they'd proven to be good at together.

But it wasn't enough for him. He knew himself better than that. He was an all-or-nothing kind of guy, which meant he'd never be content to date her for a while like Asher had, only to be dumped. He'd rather keep things the way they were right now than to have his heart slaughtered like that.

The rumble of a vehicle approaching forced his attention back to the road. The rumble grew annoyingly louder — too loud — indicating that the driver of the rusty red low rider rolling into view had paid to install extra sound packs. Other than giving everyone else a headache from the noise, he'd never seen the point in stuff like that. However, the younger punks in town loved to rev their motors as loudly as they could, especially when they were drag racing.

The rumble of a second motor alerted him to the fact that a racing challenge was likely forthcoming. He scowled at the neon yellow sports car speeding up to ride abreast of the red low rider. Main Street was a two-lane road, for crying out loud, which meant one of them was in the wrong lane. Plus, it was broad daylight.

He scanned the area, trying to catch a glimpse of either policeman that the small town employed. Unfortunately, there was no sign of a patrol car. He glanced back toward the spot on the sidewalk where Jade had been chatting with Richard. He was no longer with her. She was heading to her car with her cell phone pressed to her ear.

To Beldon's alarm, she stepped off the curb to move around the front of her car right as the drag race was beginning. It wasn't until she reached the driver's door that she must have registered the fact that she was about to have a front row seat to a drag race.

He laid on his horn, trying to distract the punk drivers from their shenanigans. However, they were beyond hearing anything other than the rumble and screech of their motors as they burned rubber and took off.

Beldon leaped from his truck and sprinted down the sidewalk in Jade's direction, but there wasn't enough time to reach her and pull her to safety. All he could do was watch in horror as she backed up and flattened herself as best as she could against the side of her car.

He could literally feel the blood draining from his face as he ran. *Please, God, don't let her get hit!*

The drag racers sped past her, cutting it so close

to her and her car that Beldon stopped breathing for the final few strides of his mad dash.

"Jade!" he choked, reaching her at last. "Are you hurt?" Visions of shattered bones danced across his vision as he gently gripped her shoulders. *Please assure me you're okay!*

She tipped her head up to him, staring dazedly. For a moment, there was no recognition in her gaze. Her lips were rounded in a silent scream. Then she wilted against him, twining her arms around his middle.

He cuddled her close, instinctively knowing that she needed to be held. She felt so fragile and delicate that it made his heart ache. If those blasted cars had come a few inches closer, she might not have survived.

"Will you let me take you to the hospital?" he rasped against her temple, loving the silky brush of her hair against his chin.

"I'm fine." Her voice shook. "Just a little rattled."

That made two of them. "At least let me drive you home."

"I'm not going home." She shifted in his arms, keeping her head against his shoulder while she gazed up at him. "I'm actually on my way to the airport." Her face was ashen, and she sounded pretty shaken.

Wow! The airport. Though he wondered where she was headed, he was even more curious about what thoughts were spinning behind her luminous green eyes. Her gaze always left him feeling like she was drinking him in and swallowing him whole. He was powerless to look away from her.

"Fine," he agreed gruffly. "I'll drive you there or anywhere else you want to go." The color was finally returning to her lips, making him long to dip his head closer to sample them. Her mouth was so close to his. So blasted close!

"Thanks, but I'm more than capable of driving myself." She scowled at him as her composure returned. "And don't even think about kissing me again."

Too late. He was already thinking about it. "Wasn't planning on it." But he wanted to, though. Badly.

"Good." She stabbed his chest with a finger. "Because every time it happens, we end up hating ourselves and each other afterward, and I don't have the emotional energy for that right now."

"I don't hate you, Jade." *I could never hate you.*

"Why are you even here?" Her voice was growing stronger, and she wiggled to loosen his grasp.

He let go of her, though he continued to hover until he was sure she could stand on her own again. "I was in the bank parking lot when I heard those cars revving. Looked up, saw you stepping into the street, and started running."

"Well, you shouldn't have bothered. As you can see, I'm fine." She gave his chest a light shove to put more space between them.

You weren't a few minutes ago, darlin'. He took an extra step back to give her more space, already missing the feel of her in his arms. "That was a close shave, Jade."

"It was, but I survived without so much as a scratch. You can go now."

Ouch! She was in an awful hurry to get rid of him. "I'll leave as soon as you give your statement to the police." He pulled out his cell phone, preparing to dial the station. "Those kids broke at least half a dozen traffic laws. Someone could've been killed."

"I'll handle it." She reached up to lower his cell phone to his side. "I know their parents."

"How do you plan to handle it?" Her nonchalance about the situation was more than a little surprising after what she'd just been through.

"I'm a criminal lawyer." She lifted her chin. "Trust me, I've got this."

He couldn't believe she was refusing to get the police involved. "Darlin', I know you studied prelaw, but that doesn't—"

"I also have a law degree," she interrupted coolly. "And I passed my bar exam. So, yes. That means I'm fully qualified to explain to a few local parents what's going to happen to their boys if anyone decides to press charges."

"You went to law school?" He gaped at her in silence for a moment, wondering why this was the first he was hearing about it. "I've known you my entire life. How did I miss the fact that you went to law school?" Yeah, she'd gone to Texas Tech for a few years, but she hadn't been gone long enough to earn both her undergraduate and graduate degrees.

"I think it's safe to say that there's a lot you don't know about me, Beldon Cassidy."

"I can't argue that, but law school, Jade? That's huge!" He regarded her with awe. "When?"

Her eyes began to twinkle. "I think you're forgetting that I was a dual enrollment student, so I had my associate's degree by the time I graduated from high school."

Holy cow! He'd forgotten all about her dual enrollment status. Plus, she was so smart that she'd skipped a grade.

"Then I fast-tracked through most of my bachelor's degree courses online after graduation," she continued in a bored voice. "Most people assumed I'd taken the year off to shop and party. I considered setting them straight, but I was having too much fun listening to all the speculation about how the spoiled and over-indulged only child of the Arlettas would turn out."

"You're kidding!" Though Jade was pretending she didn't care, he could tell she'd been hurt by such assumptions. *Shoot!* He was one of the people who'd shared those sentiments. "So when you left town for college, you were actually heading to grad school?"

"Ding! Ding! Ding!" She pointed at him like he'd just won a prize.

He frowned at her sarcastic tone, but didn't comment on it as another even more concerning question popped into his mind. "Did Asher know you went to law school?"

"That's a good question." Her voice turned bitter. "You should ask him sometime. That was back during our drifting-apart years. Not once do I recall him asking about my studies in his infrequent phone calls, so I felt no obligation to give him a play-by-play of what was happening in my life. I guess he was too busy figuring out how to be a ranch manager. There seriously were entire weeks he forgot I existed."

"That's not possible," Beldon growled. She was an unforgettable woman. There was no way his brother could have missed seeing that.

"You asked a question, and I answered it. I never said you would like the answer." She reached for the handle of her car door. "Goodbye, Beldon. I have a plane to catch."

He beat her to the door and opened it for her. "Congratulations, by the way."

She arched her eyebrows in confusion.

"About your law degree."

"Whatever." She sniffed and took her seat behind the wheel. "Pardon me for not being able to muster up the warm fuzzies about anything you or your brothers say to me these days. I am well aware that the only thing y'all see when you look at me is Asher's leftovers."

"That's not fair, Jade!" Beldon propped a hand over her open car door to keep her from shutting it.

"I don't hear you denying it." Her green gaze glinted angrily up at him.

"I think you're an amazing person. I always

have." That was putting it mildly, considering the number of years he'd been crushing on her.

"Right." Her lips flattened. "So amazing that you flushed our lifelong friendship down the toilet over a few kisses. Kisses, I might point out, that weren't completely my fault. You were a willing participant."

"Not that it will make you feel any better, but I mostly blame myself." He jutted his chin at her. She wasn't entirely blameless, though.

"Well, I'm tired of being punished every time our paths cross." Twin spots of red glowed high on her cheekbones.

"I'm not punishing you. I'm just not indulging your latest whim." *Which happens to be me.* He had zero interest in being the next Cassidy brother she toyed with for a while, then tossed aside. "The fact remains, you were still dating Asher the first time we kissed. That's cheating." He was disappointed she didn't see it that way. "I've had to live with the fact that I'm the guy who cheated on his own brother. I'm still living with the knowledge that I may be the reason you broke up."

Her lips twisted in disbelief. "Like I've told you dozens of times, Asher and I were already heading in that direction."

"But you might have patched things up again if I hadn't interfered."

"And then what?" She gripped her steering wheel tightly. "Can you honestly say that Asher would be better off right now with anyone besides Bella Johnson? Because I can't. I think they're perfect for each other."

"That doesn't make what we did right."

"So we made a mistake, Beldon!" She threw up her hands. "You think I don't realize that? Why else do you think I've spent so much time apologizing to you, your brothers, and your parents? It took a while, but I finally made my peace about what happened. Maybe you should do the same."

"I don't see how talking about it will change anything. That's the last thing Asher needs to find out right before his wedding." No way was Beldon going to hurt his brother that way. The guy had been through enough.

"Instead, you're going to continue treating me like dirt every time you see me, huh?"

"I don't treat you like dirt. I pretty much avoid you." *Except when you're in trouble or danger, which is way too often.*

"That's even worse," she snapped.

"I'm the reason you broke up, whether you admit it or not, Jade. Seems to me, I've done enough damage. That's why I'm staying away from you."

"Fine!" she exploded. "If you need me to grovel some more, I'll admit it. I broke up with Asher because of us. Not you. Us. There was no way I could continue dragging things out with him, considering how I felt about you after our kiss."

"If that's supposed to make me feel any better, it doesn't."

"I'm just trying to move forward, Beldon."

He gave her a hard look. "Looks like your moving forward involves What's His Face Harrington these days."

"As a matter of fact, it does." Her smile was chilly. "His name is Richard, by the way."

Beldon knew the guy's name, but he was in no mood to say it. "Are you dating him?"

"Hardly. We work together now." She tucked her hair behind her ear as she fixed him with an impatient look. "This morning, Buck Harrington offered to bring me on board as a partner, and I accepted."

Her announcement did nothing to curb the jealousy rolling like poison through his gut. The thought of her working every day next to that slicked-back attorney rubbed him every way but the right way. He had no doubt the guy would be putting the moves on her soon.

"And your first assignment is out of town. That figures." His lip curled in disgust. The ink couldn't be dry on her contract yet, and they were already acting like they owned her.

"No, this is personal. I'm taking a quick jaunt to Dallas to handle something for a friend."

His jaw tightened as he pushed away from her car. *Dallas.* The only person in town he knew was from Dallas was Asher's fiancée — the same woman Jade had been meeting with before Richard Harrington showed up. He wondered what she was up to, but he doubted she'd tell him if he asked.

"Just keep an eye out for those punks," he muttered, wishing he could think of something more suave to say. "No telling where they're headed to next." He hoped it wasn't the airport.

"I can take care of myself, Beldon." Lifting her chin, Jade started the motor and steered her car into the street.

As he watched her drive away, he replayed her words in his mind. *I've finally made my peace about what happened. Maybe you should, too.*

She made it sound like it was nothing more than a box to check on a form, but he knew better. *All you had to do was dole out a few apologies, darlin'. I'm the one who has to confess to my brother that I'm in love with you. That I fell for you long before the two of you broke up. That I was the reason you ultimately decided to end things.*

CHAPTER 4: CEMENTING A FRIENDSHIP

JADE

ON JADE'S flight to Dallas, all she could think about was Beldon. The man sure knew how to hog her head space! The way he'd run to her side during the drag race was so hot that she was still fanning her face about it. Despite all his talk about purposefully avoiding her, his feelings for her were nowhere near the cooling off point.

Her feelings for him weren't, either. It would've been so easy to let loose earlier and dive in for kiss number three while she was wrapped in his embrace on the side of the road. She had no doubt he would've poured everything he had into it, because he never did anything halfway. His guilt afterward would have crushed her, though, like it had the last two times he'd kissed her. They couldn't keep doing this. All of their tugging and pulling was eventually going to unravel her.

She couldn't believe Beldon was still hung up on the cheating thing now that Asher was about to get married. There seriously should be a clause to their stupid rule about exes that made it null and void after the brother in question got married.

Or some sort of amendment. Her legal mind spun over the possibilities. So far, though, she hadn't come up with a single idea of how to convince the Cassidy brothers to change their minds on the matter.

Sighing, she forced herself to put it on the back burner so she could form a plan of action for dealing with Jim Steering. The weather was decent and the Internet access was strong, so she was able to do a little digging into his background before her plane landed. She discovered two very interesting things. The superintendent of the school district where he worked was an old college buddy of hers, and his father happened to be on the campaign trail politicking for a city council position.

Gotcha, sucker! Getting Bella's life savings back was going to be easier than Jade had originally anticipated. Once her plane was on the ground, she rented a car and headed to the hotel where she'd reserved a room. She snatched a few hours of sleep in a king-sized bed that was unexpectedly comfortable, then rose early to finish plotting out her plan of attack against Jim Steering.

The college buddy she'd texted before going to bed had written her back. He was thrilled by her invitation to join her for breakfast, which meant phase one of her plan was percolating nicely.

Her emergency travel bag included the bare essentials for an attorney aiming to make an impression — a navy pencil skirt, white silk blouse, and her signature stilettos. Red this time. *Go big or go home, baby!* She powdered her nose in the mirror over the vanity, pulled her hair into a loose up-do, and painted her lips fire engine red.

I'm ready. She drove to the cozy cafe where she'd reserved a table for two over the phone and found her college friend waiting for her in the courtyard out front. Todd Hoffman hadn't changed a bit. He was still tall and skinny and still kept his hair clipped short on top and even shorter on the sides, a throwback to his days as a Navy SEAL.

"Wow!" He shook his head admiringly at her. "If I'm staring like a fool, it's because you look so amazing."

He didn't look half bad himself in a white button-up shirt and gray pinstriped suit that was nearly the same color as his eyes. His angular features were as tanned as she remembered, most likely from all the time he spent out on his sailboat.

She chuckled and held out a hand. "Well, that answers one of my questions. You sound like you're still single."

"Unfortunately." He shook her hand, scowling at the empty ring finger on the hand she had wrapped around the shoulder strap of her purse. "Apparently you are, too. That's a surprise. What happened to that cowboy you were lip-locking with a few years ago?"

She drew a deep breath, knowing it was time to lay her first card on the table. "Actually, he's engaged to a music teacher from your school district."

"No kidding?"

"Past tense." She smiled wryly. "She moved north to the panhandle and snapped up my ex."

He shot her a curious look as he hurried ahead of her on the sidewalk to open the door of the cafe. "I'm not yet sure if that's a good thing or a bad thing, so I'll refrain from commenting on it. Is she someone I know?"

"I'm not sure. Her name is Bella Johnson."

He shook his head. "Doesn't ring a bell. Should it?"

"I'm kind of glad it doesn't," Jade smiled in relief, "because she received a bad evaluation from her boss and left town over it, among other things." She was glad to learn that whatever Jim Steering had stuck in Bella's file wasn't bad enough to have crossed Todd's desk.

"Sorry to hear it."

They approached the hostess booth, where Jade announced, "We have a reservation for two under Jade Arletta."

The hostess, a teenager in a blue sundress with a flippy ponytail, beamed a welcoming smile at them. "Your table is ready. Follow me."

"Believe it or not, Bella's a friend of mine," Jade explained to Todd as they made their way to a booth at the far end of the room. It felt good to say that out loud. "That's why I'm here in Dallas. There's a situation with her ex-fiancé, who also works in your school district, that needs a little legal nudging to clear up before her wedding."

"Sounds interesting." Smiling quizzically, Todd waved her into the side of the booth facing the door, then slid in after her.

"You have no idea," she sighed.

"Then tell me." He draped an arm across the seat cushion behind her.

Though he wasn't touching her, she didn't miss the intimacy of the gesture. Now that she was single again, he probably considered her fair game for flirting. She bit back a sigh, trying to keep her mind on her mission.

Their waitress approached. Tossing a grin at Jade, Todd ordered for both of them. "Two unsweet teas with as many lemons as you can fit on the rim."

A chuckle escaped her. "You remembered."

"That whoever marries you is going to need to set up a tab with a citrus grove in Florida?" He snorted. "Yeah, I remember."

She sobered. "As an only child, a family is all I ever wanted. And maybe a house with a view. But I'm no longer sure marriage is what my future is about."

"Not sure if I agree. I'd marry you in a heartbeat if you asked me to," he teased.

Yep, he was definitely flirting. She strove to bring their conversation back to safer ground. "At the moment, I'm on the career route. Yesterday, I signed on as a junior partner with a local law firm."

Todd mockingly threw a hand over his tanned

forehead. "And she immediately dashes my hopes to the ground. Who's the lucky guy?" Every time he smiled, his gray eyes glinted like silver.

"Buck Harrington. He's pushing seventy and ready to retire, but he doesn't think his son is ready to run a solo practice."

"I'm definitely seeing an attorney boyfriend in your future. Way to go, you!" He winked at her, and she saw no reason to set him straight as the waitress returned with their drinks and rattled off the daily specials.

Both of them smiled with interest at her description of their Summer Feast Omelette. She described it as oozing with diced tomatoes, avocado slices, and jack cheese.

"Yes, please!" Jade sang out.

"Make it two," Todd added.

She waited until the waitress left to fill their orders before continuing with her story. "Richard and I have some clear differences, but I'm excited about the job. It'll give me less time to think about my many heartbreaking mistakes in the romance department."

"Are we back on the topic of your cowboy ex-boyfriend?"

"We are." She gave him a tremulous smile. "Our relationship was headed for the rocks. We both knew it. It was just a matter of who would swing the ax to put us both out of our misery. I was freaking out about it so bad one afternoon that I nearly had a head-on collision with one of his five brothers. In the process of making sure I was alright, we kissed and—"

"Whoa! Hold up there, beautiful." Todd's dark eyebrows rose in alarm. "Let me get this straight. You kissed the brother of the guy you were still dating?"

"I'm pretty sure I prefaced my story with the words *heartbreaking* and *mistakes*," she reminded.

"I'm not judging." He eagerly gestured for her to continue.

"It was an unexpectedly good kiss," she confessed, glancing down at the table. "Good enough to make us both feel guilty and good enough to still be hung up on it to this day."

"Uh-oh. This doesn't sound like it's heading toward a happy ending."

"It's not." She drew a deep breath. "Right before I left for the airport, he and I had another argument where he finally admitted he's been avoiding me."

"Coward!" Todd grimaced.

"More like unwavering loyalty to his brothers."

"Except for the part where he kissed you while you were still dating one of them."

"An attraction he's been refusing to act on ever since."

"Then he's an idiot," Todd said flatly. "The blithering kind with drool on his chin."

"I'm probably making him sound like one, but he's actually a really good person. That's what's making it so hard for me to move on. I really care for him, Todd. I wish I didn't, but I do. I'm kind of hoping this trip to Dallas helps paint me in a better light to him and his brothers."

Todd chuckled. "Wow! Okay. Give me a second to catch up." He removed his arm from the seat back to tick off the details with his long fingers. "Your ex is marrying one of my former employees. Her ex is a current employee of mine. And you're here to wrap him in legal knots and ultimately do what?"

"Make him pay up." It was a relief to move on to a different topic. "He owes her money." She stated a sum that made Todd whistle. "Her life savings is tied up in the house they bought together before she discovered he was cheating on her. Short version of the story is, she's getting married in two months and really needs the money back."

He nodded soberly. "What can I do to help?"

"Well, since you asked so nicely," she teased.

He rolled his eyes. "Like it isn't the whole reason you invited me to breakfast."

"It's only one of the reasons," she assured. "I would have looked you up regardless of why I came into town." It was wonderful seeing him again. Even his flirting was kind of nice. The way he looked at her and treated her made her feel beautiful and desirable again — like being herself was good enough. Not having to constantly walk on egg shells, feel guilty, or keep an apology balanced on the tip of her tongue was truly refreshing.

"I'm glad you did." His smile blazed into her. "Now tell me what I can do to help, starting with the name of the bozo you're dealing with."

"I'd rather not say." She shot him an apologetic look. "I'm not playing games. I just don't want to make the situation any worse than it is by ruining yet another person's career. I only came into town to pick up a check." She smiled wryly. "After I convince him to write it, of course."

Todd shook his head in wonder at her. "You're as beautiful on the inside as you are on the outside. It would be so easy to fall in love with you, if I ever have the luck to catch you between cowboys."

"Thanks. It's very sweet of you to say that." Jade felt a blush bloom on her cheeks. Gosh, but Todd was a charmer! He always had been and always would be. She couldn't believe he was still single.

Their waitress approached their booth with two plates balanced on one arm. Steam twirled up from the center of their omelettes.

Jade gave a squeal of delight as the woman set her plate down in front of her. "Okay, my day just got a hundred shades better."

Todd bowed his head glumly over his own plate. "I was trying to have a moment with you, and this time I lost out to a flipping omelette. I really need to up my game."

"Just stop." Jade chuckled. "You're priceless just the way you are."

He grimaced. "Is that why I'm still single?"

"The fact that you are kind of blows my mind." She wasn't kidding.

"Right back atcha." His gaze searched hers for a

moment. Then he dug into his omelette. "You still haven't told me how I can help you."

She reached for her tea glass to wash down her first bite. "I'd like to be seen with you today or tomorrow. Preferably in a setting where there are likely to be a lot of school principals present."

"I'm intrigued." He looked like he was waiting for her to continue. "Oh. That's it?"

"That's it." She gave him a beseeching look, silently begging him to understand. "Then I'll be in your debt, and you can make me pay up the next time you need a favor in return."

"I already need a favor." He took another bite.

"Really?"

He chewed and swallowed. "Uh-huh. After we attend a ribbon cutting ceremony for a new library this afternoon, I'd like to take you to a Little League game to meet my sister."

She wrinkled her forehead, trying to recall what she knew about his sister. "She's married to a SEAL friend of yours, right?" Which didn't explain why she would be present at a Little League game here in Dallas.

"She was, but he didn't make it back from his last deployment."

Jade laid down her fork with a gasp. "I'm so sorry, Todd!"

"You and me both, babe." Concern was etched across his angular features. "It's been a rough last few months, trying to raise a six-year-old by herself. He's on one of the teams playing this evening."

"Does she need any legal assistance?" Jade couldn't help wondering if his sister had run into a snag settling her late husband's estate.

"Not that I'm aware of. I just think it would be good for her to meet someone solid like you. She's a kindergarten teacher on a leave of absence until she can get back on her feet emotionally and otherwise."

"Count me in," Jade said simply. It's the least she could do to pay him back for his assistance with Bella's financial problems.

"Thanks. She'll be thrilled to see me with a smoking hot woman like you on my arm. She's afraid she's completely ruined my social life after temporarily moving in with me."

Jade laughed. "Hey, I'm blatantly using my connection with you to intimidate one of your employees, so it's fair play to use me in return."

"I was hoping you would say that. I wasn't kidding about the smoking hot part, either." His sideways glance was one hundred percent male and admiring.

She smiled gratefully at him. "The next time my ego needs a boost, I'm totally calling you."

"Don't mind if you do." He polished off the rest of his omelette and signaled the waitress for a refill on their drinks.

———

The ribbon cutting ceremony was located on the campus of the district's college preparatory magnet high school. It was a gorgeous brown brick building with tall rectangular windows and sculpted flowerbeds. More importantly, there were at least a dozen principals in attendance, including her target, Jim Steering. She'd looked up his picture online, so it wasn't hard to pick him out from the crowd.

He wore his dark hair on the longish side, probably to make up for his receding hairline, and that was no cheap suit he had on. From its lustrous blue, maroon, and black floral print, she was guessing it was Italian silk. She resisted the urge to roll her eyes when she spotted the silver pinky ring Bella had described.

"Get a load of that guy. Are your eyes hurting as much as mine?" Todd muttered in her ear, angling his head at Bella's ex.

"Definitely." She snickered but didn't say anything else, not wanting to give away the fact that they were discussing her target.

True to his word, Todd made a point of keeping her at his side while he was cutting the ribbon for the new library. Though Jade's main objective was to be in the publicity shots that would appear on the local news later that evening, she genuinely enjoyed being part of the ceremony. Opening a student library was a very worthy cause, in her opinion.

To her surprise, Bella called her on their drive to the Little League field. Jade frowned at her phone screen, worried that something was wrong. "Sorry, but I need to take this."

"Just don't say anything you don't want me to

hear," Todd teased from behind the wheel of his black Land Rover. He'd offered to pick her up from the hotel, and she'd gladly accepted since she didn't know her way around Dallas.

"Holy Toledo, Jade! I just saw you on TV!" Bella exploded. Then she lowered her voice. "Is it just a coincidence that you're rubbing shoulders with my former superintendent?"

"He's a friend, and it's all part of the plan." Jade couldn't muffle the note of glee in her voice. "I fully expect to have your check in hand by tomorrow."

Bella blew out a breath. "You are truly lethal. Remind me to stay on your good side."

"Whatever!" Though Jade tried to laugh it off, she knew Bella's assessment of her was accurate.

"Fair warning." Bella's voice dropped lower. "A certain Cassidy brother might have stomped out of the living room after seeing the footage of you with your hunkalicious friend."

Jade's heart sank. "Oh, no!" She hadn't considered the possibility of making the evening news all the way up in Chipper.

"Oh, yes. You made the breaking news headlines and everything."

Jade felt sick to her stomach, knowing it wouldn't help improve her image with the Cassidys. She could only imagine the man-slayer jokes Fox was making about her right this minute.

"Maybe it'll make a certain cowboy jealous enough to finally make his move," Bella murmured.

"Maybe." Jade knew it was more likely he would

assume she'd moved on with someone else. What a pickle! "Listen, we're heading to a baseball game, but I'll text you later, alright?"

"Oo, that sounds like fun! Enjoy yourself." Bella gave a nervous chuckle. "I'll just be sitting here on pins and needles, waiting for your next update."

"Everything is going according to plan," Jade assured. "I'll call or text you tomorrow."

"Thanks," Bella sighed. "For everything."

"I'm happy to help." Jade disconnected the line. Every word she'd said was true. It felt good to be elbows deep in helping someone, even if it didn't change the Cassidy brothers' opinion of her.

"What's the problem?" Todd eyed her in concern while she returned her phone to the pocket of her leather wristlet.

"We made the news."

He arched an eyebrow at her. "Isn't that what you wanted?"

"All the way up in Chipper."

"Ah. Is that going to be a problem with one of those cowboys you got dangling?"

"I do not have anyone dangling." She swatted him on the shoulder.

"Uh-huh. You keep telling yourself that."

They missed the start of the Little League game. When they pulled into the parking lot of the sports complex, it was to the sound of parents and grand-parents cheering themselves hoarse for the boys and girls on the field.

Todd jogged around the front of his Land Rover

to open the passenger door for her. "In case it's not obvious, baseball is a serious sport here in Dallas."

"Even in the Little League, huh?" Jade accepted his hand to assist her to the ground.

"Especially in the Little League."

The concession stand crew had a grill smoking with burgers and hotdogs. The air smelled like hickory and was punctuated by the chatter of kids of all ages. Several young tykes were playing hide-and-go seek beneath the bleachers, while a few older kids were tossing a football behind them.

"There you are!" A curvy woman with long dark hair tucked beneath a baseball cap hurried their way. She held a soda can in one hand and a hotdog in the other. Her jeans were fashionably frayed at the knees, and a striped team jersey was pulled over them.

Reaching her brother, she stood on her tiptoes to give him a kiss on the cheek. Then she turned to Jade. "I'm Ellie Roberts, Todd's sister."

"It's so nice to meet you." Jade didn't offer to shake her hand since both of her hands were full.

"It's nice to meet you, too." Ellie's dark eyes snapped with curiosity as they flitted between Jade and Todd. "My brother works such insanely long hours that I worry about him sometimes." The look she shot him was infused with adoration and concern.

His arm was casually slung around Jade's shoulders. "Keeps me out of trouble." He winked unconcernedly at her.

Ellie rolled her eyes at him, but kept talking to

Jade. "Whatever you did to talk him into coming to a game, I'm truly grateful."

"Told you," he muttered in Jade's ear as his sister finally headed back to the food stand, claiming they needed another set of hands on deck.

Jade wondered if she was purposefully making herself scarce, since her brother was going out of his way to make it appear he was on a date. In a way, he was. She and Todd had been friends for a long time, and both were still single. Since the Cassidys were probably thinking the worst of her right now, she figured she might as well relax and enjoy her evening.

This is all I've ever wanted. Jade glanced wistfully around them as Todd tugged her up the steps to the top row of bleachers. The sense of family and community surrounded them like a warm bubble. As soon as she was seated, Todd made a concession stand run and returned with plates of hotdogs and nachos to balance on their knees.

"Thank you. This is a really great way to spend an evening." Jade stared raptly at the field to see what was happening as the crack of a baseball bat rent the air.

"I'm glad you think so." A bemused smile played around Todd's wide mouth. "Wasn't sure if the cuisine or lack of air conditioning would be up to your standards."

"I grew up in the country," she reminded him.

"You're an interesting mix, that's for sure."

"What's that supposed to mean?" She waved a nacho dripping with cheese at him.

"You have multiple college degrees, and you've traveled the world, yet you seem content with small-town life."

"I am. Don't ask me to explain it, because I'm not sure I can."

"I won't. Just wanted you to know that I like the fact that you've never lost sight of where you came from. Roots are important."

As the sunset deepened to rose gold hues and purple shadows, Todd dipped his head closer to hers. "You wanna go somewhere we can neck?"

Her answering snicker was accompanied by a twinge of guilt "We're not in high school anymore. Besides…"

"I know. I know. Cowboy brother number two currently has your heart in a tangle."

"He does," she admitted quietly.

"Despite that, it's been nice hanging out with you today."

"It's been fun, hasn't it?"

"All except the part about you wishing I was someone else."

"Todd!" She stared at him, aghast. He was full of outrageous comments this evening.

"Don't try to deny it. I've flirted with you all day, and that sad look is still in your eyes."

"I'm sorry. I had no idea it was that obvious." She felt awful about bringing her personal misery along on their evening out.

"It's okay. That's what friends are for. I'm going to keep cracking corny jokes and trying to make you smile the whole time you're in town."

"Thanks for the warning." She stuck her tongue out at him.

"I'm also going to pay you a visit soon in Chipper. Might even bring my sister and her kid with me."

"Are you serious?" She swung her head his way in astonishment.

He cocked his thumb and pointed his forefinger at her like a pistol. "There we go! Finally got a real smile out of you."

She shook her head at him. He was such a sweet guy! "I would love to have you visit, but why Chipper? In light of full disclosure, we are a very tiny speck on the map, land-wise and population-wise."

"Because I recently got wind of the fact that someone in your tiny speck of a town applied for a sizable education grant."

"What for?" She normally did a better job of keeping up with what was happening in town, but this was the first she was hearing about the grant.

"On the application, they said it was for funding to start a new school district."

"Wow! Can't say I'm surprised, though."

"It's probably worth mentioning that the same Mr. Buck Harrington who just brought you on as a partner, is the one who submitted the application on behalf of your town council."

"Oh, my lands!" Jade pressed a hand to her heart

as the last piece of the puzzle fell into place. "I can tell you who's really behind this."

"You?" he inquired in a hopeful voice.

"No, I can't take credit for that. It's a woman by the name of Claire Cassidy. She and her husband, Ridge, are the ones who fought the hardest to incorporate our community, and now they're working around the clock to build its infrastructure."

"Cassidy, huh? Isn't that the same last name as your ex?"

"They're his parents. They helped raise the funds for our fire department in record time, along with a police force of two whole officers."

He looked thoughtful. "And now they're gunning to establish their own school district, which is why I'd like to pay a visit there soon."

Jade's heart did a rapid two-step. "Are you saying what I think you're saying?"

He waved his half-finished hotdog at her. "My sister could really use a change of scenery. Plus, I just found out that a former music teacher from Dallas lives there. It wouldn't be a bad start for staffing a couple of local schools."

She abruptly flipped his arm away from her shoulders and stood.

He squinted up at her. "Did I say something wrong?"

"No. I just need some extra space before I kiss you out of sheer gratitude. Didn't want to give you the wrong idea." Claire Cassidy was going to be ecstatic when she met Todd Hoffman, especially after finding out what he did for a living.

"I wouldn't complain." He smirked at her.

"With my luck, someone would catch it on camera, and I would have even more explaining to do when I return home."

"You really do care for that bull-headed cowboy, don't you?" His expression was unreadable.

"Yes. I think I'm in love with him, Todd," she wailed, more than a little disgusted with herself for falling so hard for someone who hadn't even asked her out yet. A guy who might never ask her out. "Just call me the world's biggest fool and be done with it."

"Who knows?" he returned mildly. "Maybe I can help out with that situation, too, if I pay a visit to Chipper."

"I don't see how." She shook her head helplessly.

"One word. Competition, babe."

"That's two words." She blushed at what he was implying.

"All I'm saying is, maybe he's the right guy for you. Maybe he's not. Either way, a little friendly competition won't hurt."

Unfortunately, she doubted she was going to be over Beldon anytime soon, and the last thing she wanted to do was hurt another really decent guy. She was going to have to be careful not to give Todd false hope in her direction.

———

The next morning, she paid a visit to Jim Steering's high school. He was standing outside by the flag pole, greeting students as they filed off their school buses. She could tell the moment he recognized her. Probably thinking it would be wise to schmooze with the superintendent's girlfriend, he abandoned his post and swaggered in her direction.

"Hi. I'm Jim Steering, head principal here." He thrust out the hand bearing a pinky ring. "Sorry, I didn't have the chance to introduce myself yesterday."

"I'm Jade Arletta." She smiled and shook his hand. Not wanting to spoil today's surprise, she'd made sure he didn't have the chance to speak with her at the ribbon cutting ceremony.

He cocked his head curiously at her. "Do you work for the district, Jade? I don't believe we've ever met."

"No. I'm an attorney from Chipper. Just visiting Dallas on a mission to help out a friend."

His smile disappeared at the mention of Chipper.

"My client's name is Bella Johnson, and I understand you owe her some money. I think we both know it won't be good publicity for your father's bid for city council if that bit of information gets out. Fortunately, all you need to do to make things right with Bella is pull out a checkbook."

As it turned out, the Steering family was seriously loaded. She had the exact amount of money she'd requested in hand within minutes.

CHAPTER 5: SECRETS NEXT DOOR

BELDON

BELDON ROSE an hour earlier than usual the next morning. He hadn't gotten much sleep. The television footage of Jade's visit to Dallas kept playing in his head, branding itself into his memories — her hands on the oversized set of scissors, Todd Hoffman's hands on top of hers as they cut the ribbon to celebrate the opening of the new library together, and the way she'd glanced laughingly up at him afterward.

She'd looked so much happier than she had during their latest round of bickering before she'd departed for the airport two days ago. Not to mention feminine and beautiful in her skirt and heels. And classy while hobnobbing with a bunch of big-wig city officials and school administrators. She'd been in her element.

A rising attorney like her quite simply didn't belong in the small town of Chipper. Beldon couldn't believe she'd already stayed as long as she had.

Working with the Harringtons was certainly going to give her a taste of what her life could be like if she chose to put all of her highfalutin college degrees to work. Heaven knew she could make a lot more money in a bigger town than she would if she stayed local.

The thought of her moving away was a depressing thought — enough to kill his appetite and make him decide to skip breakfast. He snatched a few water bottles from the fridge and a bag of beef jerky from the pantry to stuff in his saddlebag for later. Then he stomped across his empty living room and made his way to the hallway leading to his two-car garage.

He wasn't sure why his nose was so out of joint by the fact that Jade was finally moving on from the Cassidy brothers. It wasn't like the two of them had ever dated. She didn't belong to him and never had. It still felt like he was losing her, though.

And the only one he had to blame for it was himself. If he'd only waited a few more days before kissing her, she might've already broken up with Asher. Then he wouldn't have had to spend the rest of his life wondering if it was his fault.

Not that it would've made a difference in the long run. Jade had always been a love-'em-and-leave-'em kind of girl. Back in middle school, she'd dated just about every boy in her small class at one time or another. She'd done the same thing during her freshman year of high school and part of her sopho-more year, which was technically her junior year since the school had moved her up a grade between the first and second semesters. But her boy crazy days had ended when Asher asked her out.

He was the guy she'd dated the longest. They'd stayed together for the rest of high school and throughout her college years. The town gossips had given "that nice Cassidy boy" all the credit for curbing Jade's "wayward tendencies," and Beldon had spent the entire time they were dating wishing he was the Cassidy brother she was with.

Tripping over a pair of work boots he'd left in the doorway of the garage, he stalked to his truck. Leaping inside, he released the emergency brake and almost started rolling forward before remembering to open the garage door.

Man, he was tired! It was going to be a doozy of a day on the range, given his lack of sleep last night. Trying to get his head back in the game, he rolled his shoulders a few times as he drove down the gravel road leading to the central part of Cassidy Farm. Wide, grassy pastures stretched on either side of him. He could make out the shadowy silhouettes of cows stretched out among the Joshua trees, snoozing through the early hours of the morning.

Though it wasn't yet daybreak, a faint glow on the horizon indicated it was getting close. Beldon reached a crossroads and hung a left. That's when his headlights landed on a lone cow in the road.

"What the—?" He slammed on his brakes and skidded to a stop only inches shy of striking the creature. The Hereford cow lifted her head, grazing his bumper with her muzzle in her fear, and bellowed out a protest over the closeness of his vehicle. Then she trotted off the road and came to a halt in front of the wood slat fence.

She raised her head and bawled out another complaint at the barrier standing between her and the pasture beyond. Beldon turned his headlights off and his fog lights on to reduce the brightness, hoping to soothe the frightened creature. Reaching into the back seat for the lasso he always kept handy, he slowly opened his door and lowered himself to the ground.

"Easy there," he called as he unfurled his rope and crept closer.

The cow bellowed again and pressed against the fence in agitation. Beldon gave his rope a quick twirl and sent the lasso neatly over her head.

She fussed and drummed a hoof against the hard-packed ground a few times, but did not put up any resistance while he tethered her to the fence post.

Turning on his cell phone flashlight, he performed a brief examination of her flanks. "Well, I'll be!" He had no trouble recognizing her brand mark. She was from the Arlettas' ranch next door. "What are you doing so far from your herd?" He flipped off his flashlight and tucked his phone back in his pocket.

She bayed out a mournful response.

"It's alright." He patted her side. "I'll get you back home."

Her next moo sounded a little less upset. She

seemed to understand that she'd wandered into friendly territory.

"You're lucky you didn't encounter a coyote," he added in an equally soothing tone. *Or a whole pack of them*. They were as thick as thieves in the surrounding canyons at night.

Returning to his truck, he cut off the motor and locked his doors. It looked like he'd be retracing his steps and returning a wandering cow home instead of heading out to the range early. The quickest route to the Arlettas was by cutting across his own twenty acres. From there, he could reach their outermost pasture. They probably had a fence slat down.

In the hopes it was something he could fix quickly, he moved around to the back of his truck to retrieve a hammer from his storage bin. He slid it between his belt and waistband to hold it in place while keeping his hands free. Then he returned to the fence to untether the cow.

Keeping his lasso loosely knotted around her neck like a leading cord, he urged her onward. "Come on, girl. Let's get you back to where you belong."

She trotted obediently behind him on the grassy edge of the gravel road. Sure enough, they arrived at a break in the fence around the Arlettas' back pasture.

Once Beldon got the cow back on the right side of the fence, he gave her rump a light slap to get her trotting toward the rest of her herd. Turning back to the fence, he surveyed the damage. All three fence slats were lying on the ground.

To his relief, it didn't look like sabotage, so they weren't dealing with cattle rustlers. The break appeared purely due to weathering, which had resulted in dry rot. More than likely, the cow had brushed against the fence or backed into it while grazing, and the rotting wood had simply given way.

It wasn't an ideal solution, but the best Beldon could do was jerry-rig two of the slats together to form a single slat, which he then used to cover the break. He nailed the third damaged slat to the center of the jerry-rigged slats to form a temporary reinforcement beam. The whole section of fence needed to be replaced as soon as possible. If it was up to him, he'd do it today.

Glancing at his watch, Beldon estimated that the time it would take to pay a visit to Mr. Arletta would run him late for his shift, but it couldn't be helped. If the man didn't fix his fence, his herd would soon be strung halfway to Oklahoma. He was lucky that Beldon had found the wandering cow and brought her home before she'd become lost, injured, or worse.

Digging for his cell phone again, he dialed his oldest brother.

Asher picked up on the first ring. "Morning, sunshine!"

Beldon had enormous respect for the job he did as a ranch manager. "Hey, I've gotta situation that might run me a few minutes late."

"No problem. I'll give Fox's cage a rattle." Their

youngest brother had just returned to town from a straight two months of riding broncs on the rodeo circuit. "How long do you think you'll be gone?"

"I'm not sure yet. I found one of the Arlettas' cows wandering down the road and put her back with the herd through the same break in the fence she probably escaped from. I patched it together, but the whole section needs to be replaced."

"You'd best let Luis know right away."

"That's what I was thinking." For the sake of time, Beldon didn't mention the dry rot. However, he thought it was odd for Luis Arletta's fence to be in such poor repair. If the guy had a ranch hand being careless, he deserved to know about it. Unlike the Cassidys, who'd diversified their family business years ago into organic farming and wild honey harvesting, herding cattle was Luis's only source of income. He couldn't afford to have broken fences bleeding his livelihood all over the countryside.

"Fortunately, the lioness is out of town," Asher mused dryly. "You won't have to worry about a run-in with her."

Beldon's heart leaped at his brother's reference to the one woman in the world he couldn't stop thinking about. "Speaking of Jade, there's something I need to tell you about her." She was right about it being time for him to make his peace with what had happened between them, and there was no way he could do that without coming clean with his oldest brother about a few things.

"Bella already told me about the guy on TV that

Jade was getting cozy with. Guess it means you can finally quit worrying about her trying to drive a wedge between me and Bella."

"That's not what I need to talk to you about."

"Oh?"

"I'd rather discuss it in person."

"Uh, sure. You know where to find me."

"Yep, and there's one more thing I need to ask you."

"Fire away."

"Do you know if Tandy Arletta has been sick recently? Or gone through surgery or something?"

"No." The wariness in Asher's voice was replaced with concern. "Where did you hear this from?"

"Just got the impression she wasn't well while I was dropping Jade off at home during that snowstorm a while back. Did a little asking around, and turns out that no one has seen hide nor hair of Tandy in public for months."

"Huh!" Asher exclaimed. "Now that you mention it, Mr. and Mrs. Arletta have been keeping themselves pretty scarce lately. I assumed it was just our family they were avoiding, on account of Jade's breakup with me, but..." He let the possibilities hang in the air.

Beldon had assumed the same thing at first, but now he wasn't so sure. "I'll ask about her while I'm visiting with Luis."

"I'd appreciate that." Asher was silent for a moment. "I know things between our families have been strained lately, but the Arlettas are still good people. If they need anything, let them know we'll do whatever we can to help out."

"I will." Beldon disconnected the line. Returning to his truck, he drove to the Arletta ranch and parked in the circle drive in front of their home.

By now, the first rays of dawn were streaking across the sky, providing enough light for Beldon to observe the crispy remains of flowers in the concrete urns on the front porch. It looked like it had been a long time since they'd last been watered.

His sense that something was wrong grew. He only wished he hadn't waited an entire month to come back and check on the Arlettas.

Jogging up the porch steps, he mashed the door-bell button beside the double entry doors. Cobwebs clung to the scrollwork covering the frosted glass windows. He reached over to swipe away the worst cluster, flicking the sticky wad over the porch railing.

He could hear the thump of boots approaching from inside the house. The door swung open, and Luis Arletta stood there in a wrinkled shirt and stained jeans.

"Hey, Beldon." Looking puzzled to see who was standing there, he ran a hand through his dark, uncombed waves. "You need something?"

Beldon had never seen the guy looking so haggard. Shadows mottled the coppery skin beneath his eyes, and he was in need of a shave. Beldon's concerns shot higher. "Yes, sir." He angled his head toward the road. "Just wanted you to know that one of your cows got out. When I brought her back, I found a pretty bad break in the fence."

The Hispanic man's shoulders seemed to sag. "Guess I better go take a look at it." He reached over to grab his Stetson from the hall tree.

"I patched it together as best I could, but I reckon the whole section needs to be replaced," Beldon warned. "I've got some tools in my truck, if you'd like an extra set of hands."

"Why would you do that?" Mr. Arletta shot him a dark look as he stepped outside to the porch. "Didn't think the Arlettas were real popular with the Cassidys these days." Though he wasn't Jade's biological father, he'd been fiercely protective of her since the day he'd married her widowed mother. She'd been a toddler at the time.

"Because we're neighbors, sir." Beldon knew they were speaking of Jade, but that didn't change his answer. "You'd do the same for us."

"I reckon," the man muttered, reaching for the door handle to pull it shut.

"Luis?" a female voice called before it snapped closed.

Beldon's forehead wrinkled as he recognized Tandy Arletta's voice. What he didn't recognize was the weak, thready sound of it.

"Luis?" Mrs. Arletta called again. "Who's there?"

Clenching his jaw, Luis spoke through the crack in the door without pushing it wider. "It's one of the Cassidy boys. Says we got a broken section of fence in the back pasture. I'm going to have a look at it."

"By yourself?" Her voice rose shrilly.

"Nah. He offered to help fix it. I won't be gone long."

Realizing that Tandy didn't intend to make an appearance to say hello, Beldon jogged down the porch steps out of earshot. He hated the distance that had sprung up between the two founding families of Chipper. It hadn't always been like this between them. Once upon a time, they'd been friends.

He hopped inside his truck, started the motor, and rolled down the passenger window.

Luis ambled in his direction. "I'm going to head to the barn to grab a few things."

Beldon jabbed a thumb at his empty passenger seat. "It'll save time if you let me give you a lift."

With a grunt that could've meant anything, Luis yanked open the door and climbed inside. "My truck is in the big red barn out back."

"What about a circular saw and some spare fence slats?" Beldon wasn't interested in simply dropping off the man so they could drive separately to the site of the broken fence.

"In the white barn," Luis said stiffly. "Listen, if you need to run, I can handle this on my own."

Beldon drove past the red barn and parked in front of the white one. "It sounds like we both have stuff to get back to, sir. It'll be quicker if we knock this out together."

"So you keep saying." Though Luis shot him a curious sideways look as he leaped down from the truck, he sounded like he was unwinding a tad.

They swiftly loaded a tool box, a bucket of nails, two sawhorses, and a pile of slats in the bed of Beldon's truck. Luis disappeared inside his shop one last time and returned with the black plastic case containing his circular saw.

"This ought to do it," he huffed, adding it to the pile.

As Beldon drove to the site of the broken fence, dawn spread across the sky, brightening the world. In slow degrees, the shadowy grasses became green again, and the silhouettes of cattle blossomed into brilliant Hereford reds and whites. Cows staggered to their feet and stomped off the cobwebs of sleep, mooing a greeting to the two men as they approached with toolboxes in hand.

"Clever." Luis took one look at the patch of fence Beldon had jimmied back into place and grinned. "Your dad taught you well."

"Yes, sir, he did." Beldon's father had groomed his six sons as cowboys since they were old enough to crawl after him. After a hip injury cut his rodeo days short, Ridge Cassidy had switched to ranching and never looked back. He still walked with a limp, but he'd never let it slow him down when it came to herding, farming, and fathering.

The two men worked quickly and silently to pop off the old fence slats and pound new ones into place. It was a task they'd both performed countless times, one that didn't require a bunch of talking.

When they were finished, Luis straightened and lifted his hat to wipe his arm over his sweaty forehead. "Makes the rest of the fence look pretty shabby." He barked out a wry laugh.

Beldon mimicked his movements, fanning his face with his hat. "I could come back over this evening after my shift and we could have a go at another few sections of fence."

Luis's dark eyebrows shot upward. "I'd have figured you had a pretty gal waiting to fill your free time."

Beldon clapped his hat back on his head. "The only girl I've ever cared for that way is seeing someone else." It was his fault, of course, for pushing her away.

"Sorry to hear it." Luis shook his head in sympathy as he gathered up his tools. "Her loss." Clearly, he had no idea that Beldon was speaking of his own daughter.

Or my loss. Beldon helped load up the sawhorses and broken fence slats. "She's probably better off without me. I never went to college and don't plan to. This is all I'm ever going to be." He waved his hands in the air ruefully. "A cowboy with dirt beneath his nails."

"What's wrong with that?" Luis scowled at him.

Beldon settled behind the wheel of his truck with a grimace. He didn't know if Jade's father had a college degree and hadn't intended to insult him if he didn't. "I just meant she deserves someone with more polish, sir."

"I couldn't disagree more," Luis blustered as he rejoined him in the cab. "College doesn't make a man who he is. A degree is nothing more than a set of credentials to satisfy certain job requirements. Like becoming a lawyer the way my daughter did. Ranching, on the other hand, is different. It calls for blood, sweat, tears, and elbow grease. Mostly that last item."

"You can say that again." They shared a chuckle.

Beldon drove Jade's father back to the white barn to unload his tools.

"Just toss the old slats over by the wood pile," Luis instructed briskly. "They're dry enough to use for kindling the next time I need to get a bonfire started."

Beldon stacked them neatly on one side of the pile so they wouldn't become a tripping hazard. "What time would you like to meet back up this evening?"

When Luis hesitated, Beldon added, "I've got nothing better to do, sir."

"I reckon I'd be a fool to say no to that." Luis held out a hand. "How does seven o'clock sound to you?"

"I'll be here, sir." Beldon shook his hand. Not wanting to linger until things got awkward, he high-tailed it back to Cassidy Ranch to mount his horse. Today he was riding Scout, a reddish-brown and white spotted Mustang. He usually rotated between Scout and another Mustang named Sergeant. The two horses looked almost identical though they weren't related.

He rode Scout on the trail around the first pasture, paying more attention than usual to the state of the fence rails. Though he scrutinized each one, they all seemed in good repair. That was a relief. He eventually caught up to Fox, who was munching on a piece of straw when he drew abreast of him.

Fox gave an exaggerated yawn that was much louder than necessary. "Nice of you to finally show up."

"I had something to take care of." Beldon waved irritably at the trail behind him. "Feel free to get back to your beauty sleep. You need it. You're as ugly as sin."

Fox raised his Stetson to smirk at him. "In case you've forgotten, we look a lot alike." They'd both inherited their father's brown hair, though Fox's hair was a shade or two darker. Unlike the rest of his brothers, he wore it on the longer side. He had a reputation as a heartbreaker with the ladies, though Beldon had no idea if it was true or not. All he knew was that Fox was forever sneaking off without a word of warning to spend weeks at a time on the rodeo circuit. So far, it had been a profitable endeavor for him. He kept winning, and his various sponsors kept raising their bids in the effort to recruit him off each other.

Beldon's gaze honed in on the shiny gold buckle his youngest brother was sporting this morning. The state of Texas was etched into it with the outline of the state flag billowing in the background. A man on the back of a bucking bronco filled the foreground.

"Nice buckle." He nodded at it.

Fox shifted the piece of straw from one side of his

mouth to the other. "It's one of the eight I brought home with me this time."

Wow! "That's really something." It sounded like he'd placed first in all of his events.

"I'm good at what I do, Beldon. Someday the rest of y'all are going to quit looking down your noses at me for how I earn my living."

"What are you talking about?" Beldon frowned at him. "We're bloody proud of you, every one of us."

"You have a funny way of showing it."

"We worry about you, especially Mom after what happened to Dad." Ridge Cassidy had also been a bronc rider until the fall that had broken his hip. It was an injury that had forced him into retirement.

Fox's jaw tightened. "Not everyone was born to be a rancher."

"Never said they were." Beldon danced his horse around his cranky brother. "Just wish you'd unwad your boxers about the way we worry sometimes. Like it or not, it's part of the deal of being a family." He scanned the herd and saw no sign of trouble.

Fox snorted. "Y'all worry *all* the time."

"You're one of the lucky ones who has a family to worry about him." Beldon wasn't about to apologize for that. Seeing the stubborn set to his brother's jaw, he abruptly changed the subject. "Hey, have you heard anything lately about Luis and Tandy Arletta?"

"Nope!" Fox's answer was emphatic. "I make a habit of avoiding the entire family like the plague. Why?"

"Because their fences are in pretty bad repair, the

flowers on their front porch are dead, and Tandy refused to come to the door to say anything to me earlier."

"Like mother, like daughter," Fox muttered. "Count yourself lucky, bro."

Beldon ignored his snide commentary. "I got the impression something is wrong. Just wondering if you'd heard anything."

"I've been out of town for two months," Fox reminded.

"Yeah, but you get around."

"What's that supposed to mean?"

Beldon chuckled. "With as many women as you've dated, I figured you might've heard something."

"I just got back into town last night. Anything I'd heard would've been two months ago."

"And?" Beldon's heartbeat quickened in anticipation.

"I got nothing, bro. Haven't seen or heard anything unusual about them."

"Thanks. You're a big help."

"I try." Fox continued munching his piece of straw. "You got any food on you?"

It was a reminder that he'd been yanked out of bed at the last minute. He'd probably had no time to grab a bite to eat.

Beldon wordlessly withdrew his bag of beef jerky from his saddlebag and tossed it to him.

Fox caught it with a crow of delight and didn't seem to notice when the piece of straw fell from his mouth. "Mmm! Cassidy Farm makes the best jerky," he mumbled, filling his mouth. "I've missed this."

Instead of taking off as Beldon expected, Fox hung out until lunch time. Beldon appreciated the help. It was good to have Fox home. Despite his cocky insistence to the contrary, he was darn good at range riding and everything else around the ranch. Since he was out of town a lot, he tended to just pitch in wherever he was needed while he was home. As a result, he could literally do anything they asked him to. Beldon privately thought of Fox like the MVP of their team and sincerely hoped he would rejoin the family fold someday to take his rightful place at Cassidy Farm.

———

Beldon made his usual stop at the family store on his way back to meet up with Luis. On impulse, he picked up a few extra items to deliver to the Arlettas — two bags of beef jerky, a brisket, and some wild honey hand lotion for Tandy.

"Whoa!" Devlin's eyes rounded as he surveyed the pile of items Beldon had tossed on the counter next to the cash register. "I honestly don't remember the last time you cooked. Are you feeling alright?"

"Just ring 'em up and bag 'em, slick." Beldon pulled out his wallet and peeled off enough bills to cover the cost of the items. A quick glance over his shoulder revealed that their mother was not manning the bakery counter as usual. "And don't be stingy. I expect you to throw in a few danishes or something."

Devlin hollered at Emerson to toss together a bag of baked goods for Beldon. "Give him some extra donuts. Preferably ones with sprinkles," he added merrily. "He's trying to impress a woman."

"Quit being a punk, you little punk." Beldon glared at him, wishing they were outside so he could deliver his younger brother in his fancy jeans the wallop he deserved.

"Hey, I'm not the one hauling wild honey hand lotion home." Devlin snickered and danced out of the way when Beldon made a grab for him from the other side of the counter.

"I'm not taking it home, you moron."

Emerson joined them, tossing a white donut box on the counter. "Gave you our premium mix, bro. Who is she, and do we know her?"

Beldon snatched up the box and his two bags of purchases. "Since you insist on knowing, the only female in my life is Scout."

"Your horse?" Emerson guffawed. "Hope she enjoys the hand lotion."

Beldon left the store with a red face, inwardly vowing he wasn't going to go easy on either of them during their next brotherly wrestling match.

He tossed his packages on the passenger seat and headed for the Arlettas. Reaching their circle drive, he parked beside the porch steps. To his amazement, both Luis and Tandy Arletta were waiting for him on the front porch.

Luis was lounged in a rocker while Tandy was sitting in something entirely unexpected.

Beldon's boots ground to a halt at the base of the steps. He knew he was staring, but he couldn't help it.

Tandy was lounged in a wheelchair with a patchwork quilt spread over her knees. The turban was gone, her hair had been freshly styled, and her makeup was flawless.

"Hello, Beldon." The hands she held out to him shook a little. "Figured you'd be hungry after a day out in the field, so I made some sun tea and had Luis put together a tray of cookies."

Beldon couldn't take his eyes off her as he mounted the steps. A wheelchair? What was she doing in a blasted wheelchair? "Sounds good." His voice was gruff with emotion. "I brought a brisket to throw on the grill."

Luis stood and relieved Beldon of his packages. "Thanks," Beldon muttered, having a hard time meeting the man's gaze. "The lotion is for Tandy." He continued to walk toward her to take her outstretched hands. He silently bent over her to kiss her forehead.

"You must have a thousand questions," she sighed.

"No, ma'am. Just please assure me you're going to be alright."

She shook her head, tears misting her eyes. They were as green as her daughter's, reminding Beldon so much of Jade that his heart ached. "I wish I could give you a better answer, but no. The doctors say I have MS, and it's advancing quicker than we'd like."

Multiple Sclerosis? Beldon felt like the wind had been knocked out of him. When had this happened, and why in tarnation hadn't Jade said anything about it? Sure, they had their differences, but her mother's well-being was at stake here. Her very life!

"I'm sorry to hear it. Very sorry. I know it's not much, but you just shot to the top of this dusty cowboy's prayer list." Letting go of her fragile hands, Beldon took a seat on the plank floor, tossed his hat down beside him, and tipped his head against one of the porch columns. It was going to take a moment to absorb such heavy news.

"Thank you, Beldon. That means a lot." She reached for the pitcher of tea on the round table beside her. Her hands shook so badly, though, that Luis stepped closer to finish the pouring. He served Beldon a tall glass of iced tea.

"Thanks." Beldon gratefully accepted it. "What can I do to help?"

"Being here is enough." Tandy smiled through the mist in her eyes. "You're the first person who's come to see us since the diagnosis. I reckon it's more my fault than anyone else's. I haven't been able to bring myself to face the world again." She wrinkled her nose at him. "It's not like anyone is going to feel sorry for an Arletta when they find out." She glanced around the porch and yard. "Several of the women in town refer to our home as the Taj Mahal."

"Then tell me what needs to be done here at the Taj Mahal, ma'am."

She smiled at his attempt at a joke. "You're already helping out with the fence. I couldn't possibly ask for more." She tried to lift the tray of cookies to pass to him, but Luis had to step in again to assist her.

Beldon helped himself to half a dozen. He was famished. "There's gotta be something else I can do. Like I told Luis earlier, I don't have anything else better to do. No wife. No kids. No pets."

"We-e-ell…" She shot a doubtful look at her husband, who shook his head fiercely.

"Let's not, babe," he pleaded in a low voice. "We'll figure it out."

"Figure out what?" Beldon glanced between them.

Though Luis continued to shake his head, Tandy confessed, "It's the house."

"What about your house?" He sat up with visions of leaking roofs and broken water pipes flooding his mind.

"It needs to be cleaned from top to bottom," she sighed. "Jade's bringing some friends to town with her in a few days. She offered to pay for a cleaning service to get the place ready, but I don't want any of the women in town to see me like this. Not yet."

Friends. Beldon's heart sank, wondering if the fellow on television would be included with Jade's guests.

"I think his silence speaks for itself." Luis's dark

eyes twinkled. "How about we just let the boy stick to mending fences?"

"No, I'll do it." Beldon grinned as another thought struck him. "I was just imagining Jade's reaction if she found out. She and I aren't on the best of terms right now."

"She'll just be grateful to come home to a clean house," Tandy assured quickly.

"Please don't tell her I had any part in it." Beldon curled to his feet. "If she finds out, she'll take off my head, and there will be a far worse mess to clean up."

"It'll be our secret." Tandy looked enormously relieved. "We'll pay you, of course."

"I'd rather just pitch in and help out Luis." From the looks of things around the ranch, the Arlettas were likely a little strapped for cash. "Mom made sure us boys know how to push around a vacuum and mop, but I can't promise that my bachelor cleaning skills are up to your expectations."

"At least stay for dinner tonight," she pleaded. "That's a mighty big brisket you brought us."

"Now you're talking my language." He pretended not to listen while she and Luis hammered out a game plan for how to make dinner happen while he was away repairing fences.

"I may be in a wheelchair, but I can still flip meat on a grill," she fumed. "Go! I insist."

Beldon's chest wrenched with sympathy. Man! What Tandy was dealing with right now was tough! The poor woman was fighting to maintain the basic physical movements that most people took for granted.

Inevitably, his thoughts returned to Jade. He could only imagine how hard it was for her to watch her mother's downward spiral. It didn't explain why she'd taken off to Dallas to hang out with friends — now of all times — but it did explain why she'd finally gotten a paying job. When word got out about her family's health and financial problems, there were people in town who would probably gloat that her life as a diva was over.

All Beldon felt was a dull ache in his chest on her behalf. He was thankful he lived only a stone's throw away. In the coming days, it would make it that much easier to check in on her and her parents.

CHAPTER 6: BIG FAVORS

JADE

JADE STARED out the window of Todd's Land Rover, anxious to be home again. She hadn't meant to be gone for four days, but it had taken a whole day for Ellie to pack. Packing for her son, Jackson, was about more than throwing clothes and toys into suitcases. He suffered from asthma, and she'd needed to contact Jackson's doctor to secure a refill on his prescription for his inhaler. As a very energetic little athlete, it wasn't something they wanted to risk traveling without.

Jade had considered sticking to her schedule and flying home ahead of them. However, Todd's offer to drive and save her the cost of a plane ticket was hard to pass up, especially since her mother was having a good week healthwise.

Lingering an extra day in Dallas, however, meant it was taking longer to deliver Jim Steering's check to Bella. Jade was sort of dying to see Bella's expression when she finally had the check in hand. Bella had already texted at least a dozen OMGs over the news that her life savings was en route.

A shrill whistle blasted through the vehicle from the backseat, jolting Jade from her thoughts and making her whirl around.

"Oh, Jackson!" his mother wailed, leaning over to swipe a green plastic kazoo from his mouth. "Where did you get that?"

"From Jason's birthday party," the six-year-old chortled, puckering his lips around the noisemaker to give it another blow. "Found it in my backpack."

Ellie didn't look too happy with his answer, so Jade hid her smile as best she could and turned back around.

There was another muffled hoot of the kazoo before Ellie succeeded in wrestling it away from her son. "Lord, give me strength," she muttered beneath her breath. She leaned forward to rest her hand on the top of Todd's seat. "Y'all are so sweet to put up with my single mom drama here in the backseat. I wouldn't blame you if you kicked us out and made us walk the rest of the way."

Todd grinned at her through the rearview mirror. "No can do, sis. We're still thirty miles from Jade's place, and it's 103 degrees outside. You'll just have to muscle through back there."

"It was really sweet of you to bring us along." She settled back in her seat and reached over to ruffle Jackson's hair. "I can't remember the last time we took a vacation."

"Mom!" he protested, scooting as far away from

her as he could in his booster seat. "I'm not a baby anymore!"

This time, Jade was unable to hide her mirth. The kid was so stinking cute! "Your nephew is a pistol," she chuckled, tapping Todd's shoulder with her fist. "Reminds me of someone else I know."

"No idea what you're talking about." He sobered as he turned his head to catch her eye. "For the last time, are you sure it's okay to pile in on your parents like this?" He was referring to her mother's condition, of course.

Her smile faded. "I'm very sure. Mom has good days and bad days, but I honestly think it'll do her good to have company. It'll take her mind off of… things." Or so Jade hoped. Outside of a miracle, her mother wasn't going to get any better.

"If you change your mind, we have no problem transferring to a hotel." Ellie shuddered. "There's no telling what other surprises my son might have brought along."

"Oh, she loves kids. Mark my words, she is going to thoroughly enjoy having Jackson scampering through the house." Jade smiled over her shoulder at Jackson, who was making flying sounds and pretending to zoom an airplane through the air. "Plus, I can guarantee you'll like our guest rooms much better than the little motel on Main. There's nothing like waking up to a view of the canyons."

"I can't wait. We haven't been this far north in, like, forever." Ellie's eyes took on a sad, faraway look that told Jade she was probably remembering when Jackson's father was alive.

The next several miles passed in relative silence. Apparently, it was time for Jackson's favorite kids' show, which Ellie was able to tune into via a movie app. She slipped headphones over her son's ears and let him watch it on her cell phone. Then she reclined her seat and closed her eyes, presumably to catch a cat nap.

Todd leaned on his armrest to speak in a low tone to Jade. "Thanks for arranging my appointment with Claire Cassidy. I'm really looking forward to exploring my options up here in Chipper."

Wondering if he was referring to something other than his career, she searched his strong profile.

He caught her staring and winked at her. "Yeah, I was including you in those options. If that range rider crush of yours doesn't cowboy up soon—"

"Todd!" she hissed with a warning nod at the back seat.

"Chill. He's got a headset on."

"It's not glued to his head." Jade shot Todd a warning look. "They could come off at any second, and underneath them are a pair of small ears in the backseat that don't miss much."

"My ears aren't that small," Jackson muttered.

She looked over her shoulder in astonishment to discover that the headset was now resting down around his neck. "Point made," she stage whispered to Todd.

He winked at her again.

"Why do you keep winking at her, Uncle Todd? You don't wink at me that much."

Ellie abruptly sat up in her seat. "Jackson, honey, let's finish your show, shall we?" She reached over, intending to return the headset to his ears.

"I have a better idea. Look up here, Jax." His uncle tapped the rearview mirror. As soon as Jackson complied, he proceeded to give one exaggerated wink after another. With each wink, his expression grew sillier. In no time, Jackson was howling with laughter.

The city line of Chipper came into view with a simple green sign on the side of the road.

"Almost there." Jade's heartbeat sped with apprehension at the thought of seeing her mother again. *Please, God, don't let her be any worse.* She turned toward the window so no one would see the dampness glistening in her eyes.

Moments later, they were bumping up the gravel drive leading to her parents' ranch. The familiar roof line popped into view, along with the towering Redbuds, Cedar Elms, and Junipers clustered on both sides of the house.

"You live in a castle, Miss Jade!" Jackson pressed his face to the window, staring wide-eyed up at the second and third-story balconies. "Are there any ghosts in it?"

"Not a single one," she assured cheerfully.

"What about an ogre?"

"No ogres, either." His face fell, making her chuckle.

"Any dragons?" he asked hopefully.

"Now Jackson," his mother cut in. "I've told you a thousand times that dragons are only in storybooks."

"Bummer, huh?" Jade made a comically sad face at him. He hooted with laughter, and peace was restored.

Todd steered his SUV around the circle drive and parked behind a silver pickup that was parked directly in front of the porch steps.

Jade gripped her seat rests, immediately recognizing the truck. What in the world was Beldon Cassidy doing at her parents' house?

Todd reached over to squeeze her hand. "You okay?"

She jumped at his touch. "I, ah…yes. I'm great!" She reached for her purse and briefcase, smiling brightly to mask her jangled nerves. "It's good to be home." Not waiting for him to get out and come around to her side of the vehicle, she pushed open the door and dragged in a few bracing gulps of air.

The front doors of her childhood home swung open, and her father pushed her mother's wheelchair onto the porch. "There's my favorite daughter!" he cried, holding out his arms to her.

Jade smoothed her hands down her wrinkle resistant green silk blouse and pasted on her brightest smile. "Hi, Dad! Hi, Mom!" She had on a pair of designer blue jeans tucked into high-heeled black boots, so she had to tiptoe across the driveway to avoid scratching the heels in the gravel.

She hurried up the porch steps and bent over her mother's wheelchair to kiss her on the cheek. "Missed you."

"I missed you more." Tandy Arletta reached up to cup her daughter's face in her hands.

Jade could feel her fingers tremble against her cheeks. "How are you feeling today?"

"Better now that you're here. Go on and introduce us to your friends."

"I will as soon as they make it to the porch." Jade straightened to throw her arms around her father. She hugged him tightly. "You holding up okay?"

The skies were turning rosy, and the smell of hickory smoke was in the air, telling her he had meat grilling on the back porch for dinner.

"I am, but I reckon I mostly owe it to Beldon Cassidy."

"Why's that?" She frowned. "I see his truck. What's he doing here?"

"A little bit of this. A little bit of that," her mother chimed in merrily. "He checks in on us just about every day."

"Really?" Jade stared at her parents. *Since when?* She knew for a fact that he'd been purposefully avoiding her and her family for months!

Her father waved a hand like it was no big deal, though his expression was a bit sheepish. "One of our cows got out. He found a broken section of fence while he was bringing her home and helped me fix it. We've been tinkering on the fences together ever since."

So, Beldon was here, keeping an eye on things the whole time I was out of town. It couldn't be a coincidence. She resisted the urge to press her hands to her chest. "That's really nice of him." She strove to keep her voice casual, not wanting her parents to sense how much the news had shaken her.

She'd told him in no uncertain terms to mind his own business, and he'd refused — just like she'd refused to stay out of Bella's business. Either he was purposefully needling her, or he'd actually been telling the truth when he claimed he still cared about her and her family.

Her father's sharp look told her that she didn't quite succeed in keeping her expression nonchalant. He slid an arm around her shoulders, keeping his voice low. "I know things are a little tense at the moment between us and the Cassidys, but he was just trying to be neighborly. I hope that's not going to be a problem."

"Of course not." She squared her shoulders. "Why would it be? Like you said, he's a neighbor."

"He's a good neighbor," her mother corrected firmly.

"I'm glad to hear it." She watched as Todd lugged a double pair of suitcases to the porch in one hand while his other hand remained like a vise around one of Jackson's ankles. His nephew was riding on his shoulders, hollering "Giddy-up!"

Hurrying toward them, she removed the suitcases from his hand and set them on the porch. "Mom, this is my friend, Todd Hoffman. We met in college. Like I told you over the phone, he's busy wowing out the education system in Dallas with his trail-blazing superintendent policies."

Todd slid Jackson from his shoulders before stepping forward to shake her parents' hands. "Really appreciate you extending your hospitality to my sister and me." He gestured at her to join him on the porch. "This is Ellie, and this is Jackson."

She hurried up the steps with two more suitcases in hand. Jackson promptly hid behind her legs and started playing peek-a-boo with no one in particular.

Ellie gazed down at him affectionately. "If my son gives you any trouble, we can throw him out in the barn for the night." He squealed in alarm and ducked farther behind her legs.

Tandy smiled warmly. "We have a few barn cats who wouldn't mind the company."

"Cats!" Jackson clapped his hands and stepped out of his hiding place. "Where?"

"They'll come around," Luis assured, squatting down in front of him. "You just gotta keep an eye out for them." He turned to point out the barns. "There's one now, peeking at us from the loft. Can you see it?"

Ellie stepped around them to shake Tandy's hand. "It's so nice to finally meet you. Jade told us all about you on the way here and assured us that you like kids. That said, I'm going to apologize in advance for all the noise, trouble, pranks, and any more kazoos he may have snuck into his backpack."

Tandy watched Jackson in fascination. "No apologies necessary. We haven't had this much excitement at the ranch for years. It'll be better than TV."

Jackson abruptly glanced over at her. "Why do you have wheels on your chair?"

Silence settled over the porch, making Jade regret that it hadn't occurred to her to explain to the kid ahead of time what a wheelchair was.

Tandy Arletta merely wagged a finger at her husband. Adopting a mischievous look, she explained, "It's so I can race Mr. Arletta to the kitchen." She dropped her voice to a conspiratorial note, leaning closer to the boy. "He and I like the same cookies, so I have to get a head start, and these wheels," she gave them a firm pat, "really help."

"Cool!" he breathed in awe. Tipping his head up at Ellie, he begged, "Mom, can I have a chair with wheels? Please, please, please!"

Everyone laughed, and the tension in the air evaporated.

Jade's father helped carry the last of the suitcases inside while Todd rode Jackson around the driveway a few times on his back.

"Alright now, you little varmint." After spinning him around until they both were dizzy, he returned him to his feet, chuckling when the boy had trouble standing up straight. "Well, go on! Help your mama unpack, you hear?"

Jackson wobbled around for a few seconds, enjoying the dizzy effect until it wore off. Then he shot like a race horse into the house, yelling, "Mo-o-om! Where are you?" at the top of his lungs.

Todd shrugged sheepishly at Jade. "At least Ellie warned them."

"My parents are going to have the time of their lives with him around," she assured. "They've joked my entire life about how many grandkids they expect from their only child." At the rate her dating life was going, though, their optimism was surely waning.

"I wouldn't mind a few rugrats of my own someday." Todd reached out to tweak her nose. "Do you want kids, or is it only wishful thinking on your parents' part?"

"I do." Jade wasn't really in the mood to discuss her ticking biological clock. She had too many other things to worry about right now — her mother's illness, her new job that would be starting on Monday, and whether she would run into Beldon Cassidy before he drove off in his truck. She hadn't expected him to make an appearance so soon after her return to town and wasn't sure what she would say to him.

Todd studied her quizzically for a moment. "Want me to take your suitcases inside?"

She blinked at the question, realizing she'd temporarily zoned out on him. "Sure. That would be great. My room is upstairs. Hang a left. It's the last door on the right." She hoped he'd remain inside to get settled in, preferring to be alone when Beldon made it back to his truck.

"Consider it done, beautiful." No sooner had Todd disappeared inside, than Beldon strode around the side of the house from the direction of the barn.

It was almost as if he'd been waiting for Todd to leave. His steps slowed as he approached her. "You're home."

"I am. I wasn't expecting to see you here." She drank in the sight of his broad shoulders, liking the way his navy blue t-shirt hugged his chest. He had a lighter blue and red plaid shirt tossed over it like a jacket, with the sleeves rolled up and the front unbuttoned. His jeans and boots were dusty as if he'd just come in from the field.

His jaw tightened at her words, though his Stetson was tipped so low over his eyes that she couldn't see his expression. "One of your cows got out, and I brought him back."

"Dad told me." She instinctively stepped closer to him, then stopped when she realized what she was doing. "It was really kind of you." There was a time she would've walked straight into his arms and hugged him, but that time seemed like eons ago.

"Why didn't you tell me about your mom?" he demanded curtly.

Her shoulders stiffened at his swift change of subject. "She didn't want anyone to know." She eyed him worriedly. "Please assure me you haven't told anyone else."

"It's not my news to tell."

"Does your family know?" she pressed.

"If they do, they didn't hear it from me."

"So, you've not heard them talking about her?"

"No, but you should probably tell them soon.

Word is bound to get out eventually. Seems to me it would be best if they heard it from you."

She bit her lower lip, knowing he was right. She was immensely grateful that he'd kept it to himself up to this point. "So, have you talked to Asher yet? About us?"

His blue gaze flared at the word *us*. "I told him there was something we needed to discuss about you, but that it needed to be done in person."

"And?" She held her breath.

"Haven't been able to catch him alone yet. I've been spending every spare second..." He glanced away from her. "I'll get around to it eventually."

Her eyes widened as it dawned on her what he'd started to say. "You've been spending every spare second over here helping my parents, haven't you?" That would explain the freshly mowed and trimmed yard. Her dad kept it mowed, but he hadn't trimmed or edged it in ages.

Beldon pushed back his hat to scowl down at her. "I'm not the monster you think I am."

"I know you're not." Wistfulness gripped her. "That's why I'm so anxious for you to speak with Asher about us. I want you back. Our friendship. Everything we had before."

His gaze locked with hers for a long, breath-stealing moment. "I'm not sure we're going to be able to put that cat back in the bag, Jade."

"I'm asking you to be my friend again," she pleaded. "Is that a no?" She was weary of being at odds with him. She wasn't sure how much more her heart could take.

"I'm not sure that I can."

"Okay." She blinked as a rush of disbelieving tears filled her eyes. Beldon had never been this cold with her before. "Then I guess this is goodbye." Her voice broke.

"That's not what I meant."

"It's what you said." In a burst of blind anger, she closed the distance between them. "For old times' sake," she snapped, resting her hands on his shoulders and standing on her tiptoes to press her lips against his.

Warmth shot through her when his hands moved to her waist, and his mouth moved hungrily over hers. It was as if he had no willpower to resist her even though he wanted to, which only pushed the cracks in her heart wider.

"Jade," he muttered hoarsely, reaching up to capture her face with one dusty hand. "Look at me."

"No," she choked, wrenching away from his grasp. "I can't do this anymore." Whirling, she ran blindly toward the barn, no longer caring if the gravel scratched the heels of her boots.

"Jade, please!" Beldon called after her. There was an urgency in his voice that she'd never heard before.

She didn't turn around. She couldn't. Reaching the horse barn, she climbed up the ladder to the loft and collapsed face down in the hay.

There was a painful stretch of silence outside before she heard the rumble of a truck motor. She listened, hardly breathing, until he drove away. Then she wept and wept and wept.

It was a long time before she could compose herself enough to make it back to the house. She crept through the back door, picking hay out of her hair and praying she wouldn't run into anyone. She could hear voices coming from the living room in the front of the house — Jackson's high-pitched chatter, Ellie's chuckle, and Todd's humorous baritone. Her mother's trembly laugh joined in.

"Are you alright?" Her father's voice made her jump as she moved toward the back stairs.

"Oh!" She squinted across the den to find him standing alone by the window. There were no lights on in the room. "I didn't see you there."

"I'm worried about you." He beckoned for her to join him at the window.

She moved across the room and sank gratefully against him, reveling in his unique dad smell. Her nose picked out overtones of hay, hickory smoke, and the grand outdoors.

He hooked an arm around her to anchor her more securely against his side. "You want to tell me what's really going on between you and Beldon Cassidy?"

"No," she murmured damply, wondering if he'd witnessed her encounter with Beldon. She turned her face to bury it against his shoulder and started crying again.

Her father simply held her, gently rubbing one large hand up and down her arm. He didn't speak until she grew still again. "It occurred to me that a boy who checks in on your parents as often as he does must care very much for my daughter."

She shuddered at his words, not sure how to answer him. Her sobbing had left her weak and drained.

"Then it occurred to me that the reason you and Beldon are this much at odds with each other is because something already happened between you. I wasn't sure until I saw you together outside this evening."

"Dad, please!" Her voice shook. "Don't. I'm begging you."

"Okay." He hugged her tightly, pressing a kiss to the top of her head. "I've just never seen you this worked up over anyone before. Not even Asher, despite all the times you two broke up and made up." He chuckled wryly. "And broke up and made up some more. Liked to give me whiplash."

"I don't want to talk about it." She sniffled loudly. "Just please warn me the next time Beldon is coming over, so I can be someplace else."

"If you insist." He gazed down at her, looking troubled.

"Thank you." She shifted in his arms. "I need to beg one more favor of you and Mom."

"What is it, hon?"

She smiled despite her misery, unable to remember the last time the man had ever said no to her. He'd adored, cherished, and spoiled her rotten straight through to adulthood. "I'd like to add another friend to our guest list for dinner this evening." She didn't want to risk running into Beldon again if she drove to the Cassidys. However, Bella deserved to receive her settlement check from her ex as soon as possible.

"Sure thing, kiddo. I'll let your mother know."

"Thank you." She gave him another hug before slipping from his embrace and heading up to her room. It was going to take a warm washcloth over her eyes and tons of makeup afterward to make her face presentable enough to return downstairs.

After texting Bella an invitation to dinner, she stepped into a steamy shower to wash off the cramped and wrinkled feel of riding inside a vehicle for so many hours. Then she donned a simple white sundress with spaghetti straps. She blow-dried her hair and kept it down, allowing it to cascade in soft waves past her shoulders. Lastly, she applied a clever mix of makeup to mask the shadows beneath her eyes and the splotchiness on her cheeks. There wasn't much she could do for her red-rimmed eyes, other than hope the redness would fade soon.

Spinning toward the window to soak in the canyon view, she allowed her mind to drift to more practical matters. It was a good thing Mr. Harrington was in the position to bring on a junior partner, because her family's bills were piling up fast. Sure, their insurance covered her mom's doctor's visits, but it didn't cover her and Dad's new king-sized bed, which boasted split mattresses that reclined on both ends. Or the massage chair. Or the bathroom renovation with the walk-in bathtub. Or the ramp leading from the side yard to the porch. The lists of upgrades to accommodate her mother's worsening medical condition went on and on. Though her mother fussed about all the trouble they were going to on her behalf, Jade was just as determined as her father to provide her every comfort available.

In fact, Jade was the one who'd insisted on the home nursing visits. She realized it was the only way her father was ever going to be able to get back to ranching. She respected his wish to spend every moment he had left with her mother, but there were fields to plant, cows to fatten up, and fences to mend — whole acres of them. Her mother's illness was their new way of life now. They were slowly figuring out how to balance it along with their other responsibilities. Like her mother reminded them every day, they still had to keep on living.

It was huge of Beldon to be pitching in the way he was. There wasn't anything else he could have done right now that Jade would have appreciated more. She could tell that his help meant a lot to her father, too. Still, she was glad to be starting her new job on Monday. Hopefully, her work schedule would minimize the number of encounters between her and Beldon going forward.

As the dinner hour approached, she reluctantly spun away from the window to buckle on a pair of strappy gold sandals. Then she made her way down the front set of stairs. Todd met her at the base of them.

To her surprise, he was in a black and white plaid

shirt and jeans. A fancy silver belt buckle anchored his belt, and black snakeskin boots encased his feet.

"Um...wow!" She gaped at him.

He spread his hands, grinning lazily at her. "When in Rome..."

"Or Chipper, which is infinitesimally smaller, but sure." She playfully linked her arm around his and tried to tug him toward the dining room, but it was like trying to move a tree that had grown roots through the floor.

His gray gaze raked her features. "First things first. Are you alright?"

"Perfectly alright," she lied, hoping her eyes were no longer red.

"You don't have to pretend with me, Jade." He gave her arm a gentle squeeze. "Not trying to climb up into your business, but I couldn't help noticing how long you were missing after a certain silver pickup drove away."

She gave him a tight smile. "Beldon and I are working through some things. That's all."

"From my angle, all he did was make you cry again."

"Believe it or not, I can't blame him for that." She'd been the one to initiate their kiss.

"You're right. I don't believe it."

She felt guilty about painting Beldon in such a bad light. "He's actually been doing a lot around the ranch in my absence. My dad is really grateful to him."

"A point to the competition, but I'm not looking

for reasons to like him, in case that escaped your notice." Todd studied her with bemusement.

Though she gave a short chuckle, worry gripped her. "Please assure me again that your primary reason for visiting Chipper is to explore a career opportunity." *Not in the hopes of catching me on the rebound*.

"It is, but getting to visit with you and your family is a big side perk. Not gonna lie."

"Right back atcha. I just don't want your trip to become more about me than your job. I'm not ready for that, and I value your friendship too much not to be perfectly honest up front."

"Ouch! The dreaded friend zone conversation."

"What few friends I have left are very important to me, Todd. I can't afford to lose another one because of crossed wires and mixed messages."

"You won't lose me. I happen to appreciate brutal honesty."

"Me, too." *From everyone except Beldon, as it turns out*. Jade squeezed Todd's arm. "So, are you ready to meet my ex's fiancée? She's pretty wonderful."

"I am." He shook his head, grinning. "You really do lead a more exciting life than I do. I feel old and dull in comparison."

"Whatever." Jade genuinely longed for the day when the drama in her life would calm down a little.

As they entered the dining room together, her mother glanced up happily. "Finally! Someone found my sweet girl." She beamed her highest wattage smile at Todd. Jade hoped it wasn't as obvious to everyone else present as it was to her that Tandy was back to her old tricks — assessing every guy under the age of forty as a potential boyfriend for her only daughter.

Luis's expression was noncommittal as he silently took note of the hand Jade had tucked through Todd's arm. He was seated at the head of the table with his wife's wheelchair parked on his right. Ellie was sitting across from Tandy with Jackson wiggling at her side, pointing out all the foods he wanted added to his plate. It looked like Luis had catered in some side dishes to go with the platter of meat he'd pulled off the grill.

Bella, who'd been perched on the chair next to Tandy, rose with a squeal of delight at the sight of them. "My hero!" She walked toward Jade with her arms outstretched. She looked more like a teenager in her jeans and braids than a full grown woman about to get married.

"He didn't put up much of a fight," Jade murmured in her ear as they hugged. Then she passed over the precious check.

"Only because you had him outflanked with multiple cannons pointed at his head." After a dazed look at the amount written on the check, she folded it and stuck it in the back pocket of her jeans. "I couldn't believe it when the bill of sale for our home showed up in my email inbox a few days ago. For my portion of it, anyway. I've never in my life been happier to sign off on something. My shoulders feel about two thousand pounds lighter."

"I enjoyed being back in the game." Jade had missed practicing law. There was no feeling in the world better than helping the downtrodden receive the justice they deserved. "Besides, it was good practice for what I'll be facing on Monday."

Jade claimed the chair beside Bella, leaving the one at the foot of the table for Todd. She was glad they weren't sitting side-by-side, not wanting to give the impression to those present that the two of them were a couple...or one in the making. He was such a great guy, but her heart wasn't available. It just wasn't.

Her father said grace, and everyone started passing the food. There were two enormous bottom round roasts on the table, surrounded by bowls of steaming vegetables. There were tiny red-skin potatoes, carrots in a rainbow riot of colors, sautéed string beans, and ornamental baby squash. Jade quickly revised her opinion of where the side dishes had come from. They weren't catered in. On the contrary, they'd come from the prized gardens at Cassidy Farm.

This was Beldon's doing. There was no end, it seemed, to his generosity. She nibbled on her food, but had a hard time working up an appetite. It unnerved her to realize that this was going to be her life going forward. Everywhere she looked reminded her of him — the mended fences, the feast in front of her, even Bella.

While she pretended to eat, she listened to Bella strike up a conversation with Ellie. As school teachers, they had a lot in common and were soon swapping classroom stories.

At one point, Bella laughed a bit shamefacedly. "Sorry. Sometimes I get carried away when I meet a fellow teacher. I didn't realize until just now how much I miss being in the classroom."

"Enough to consider going back?" Todd raised his eyebrows at her.

At her deer-in-the-headlights look, Jade leaned her elbows on the table. "Oh! That reminds me." She shot Bella a smug look. "A certain principal, whose name will not be named, has not only cleared your employee file of his previous complaint, but has additionally placed a glowing recommendation in it."

Bella looked stunned. "You did this?" she gasped. "For me?"

"All I did was provide him with a little encouragement."

Bella looked like she was about to expire from happiness. "In that case, Mr. Hoffman, my answer is yes. I would love to return to the classroom." Before returning to Cassidy Farm after dinner, she pulled Jade aside on the front porch. "I honestly don't know how to thank you."

"Just make Asher happy." Jade couldn't shake the sense of finality she felt as Bella prepared to depart. She'd never stopped caring for the Cassidys. But like Beldon had said, things weren't going back to the way they were before. It was time for her to accept that.

"I'll do my best, but I wish there was something I could do for you in return." Concern swept across Bella's heart-shaped features.

"I did what I did as a friend," Jade reminded. "There are no strings attached."

"But I like strings," Bella joked. "Pardon the guitar humor, but it's true. Despite the rocky start to our friendship, I'm enjoying getting to know you. Honestly, it feels like having a superhero in my court."

"Oh, please!" Jade searched her features, wondering why she was still standing on the porch. She seemed hesitant to leave.

"I know it's a little crazy for us, of all people, to become friends," she burst out suddenly, "but we have. For real. And that's worth something to me." Her voice dropped to a low, earnest note. "Do you have any idea how many women in this town hate me for wandering in with nothing more than a guitar to my name and ending up with a rock on my finger?"

"I have a pretty good idea." Jade nodded knowingly. That same group of women hadn't been too thrilled with how long she'd kept Asher Cassidy off the single and available list during high school and college. Sure, they still came to her when they needed events organized, but they weren't her friends and never would be.

"Duh! Right. Well, add that to the fact I have no family, there's probably not going to be much of a wedding party."

Jade frowned at the shriveled up plants in the flowerpots on her parents' front porch. They needed to be replaced. "What do you mean?"

Bella threw up her hands. "No mother, no sisters, and no friends mean no bridesmaids." As she caught Jade's eye, her expression grew stricken. "Sorry. I shouldn't have said no friends. I have you now. And Ellie, too, though she'll probably head back to Dallas soon." She stepped impulsively closer, eyes growing wide. "Oh, my goodness! Are you thinking what I'm thinking?"

"Probably not." She had no earthly idea what the flushed bride-to-be was thinking.

"Then I'm just going to say it. You're going to think I'm crazy, but will you be my maid-of-honor?"

"Bella!" A dozen protests sprang to Jade's lips. "I'm not sure that's a good idea." Correction. She was very sure it wasn't.

Bella recoiled a few inches, wrapping her slender arms around her waist. "You're more than welcome to say no, but it's my choice to ask you."

"Of course it is!" Jade hadn't meant to hurt her feelings. "And if it was just our friendship at stake, I would say yes in a heartbeat." She pressed a hand to her chest, unable to picture herself being escorted down the aisle by Asher's best man. She had no doubt it would be Beldon Cassidy. "But there are the feelings of no less than eight Cassidys to consider."

A giggle bubbled out of Bella. "Five of whom may want to shoot both of us if you say yes."

Jade tried to muffle an answering giggle, but

failed. "You're right about one thing. I think you're crazy for asking me." She wanted to say yes, though. Oh, how she wanted to!

Bella grew serious. "You're the only reason I can even afford my wedding dress. Without your help…" She stopped and shook her head. "Seriously, Jade, I'd be picking wildflowers off the side of the road and making cupcakes from a box mix."

"You call it help, but the Cassidys will call it interference," she warned. *Gosh!* She was so tempted to just accept Bella's offer and be done with it.

"Not Asher." Bella lifted her chin. "When he sees the check in my pocket, he's going to be as kiss-the-ground grateful as I am."

"Beldon, on the other hand, will crack in two when he finds out. About me, not the check. He warned me, in no uncertain terms, to keep my nose out of your wedding plans."

"What?" Bella stormed. "I can't believe he ever considered it his place to say that to you! It's our wedding. Not his."

"To be fair, I think his biggest concern at the time was that I was secretly scheming to sabotage your relationship with Asher."

"If I thought there was any chance of that, I would've challenged you to a mud wrestling contest instead of asking you to be my maid of honor."

Jade burst out laughing. "How can I say no to a colorful woman like you?" She briefly squeezed her eyelids shut as she imagined the resistance they would receive from the Cassidys on the matter.

"Granted, Beldon may spew like a volcano when he finds out he's escorting me down the aisle, but I am suddenly okay with that."

Bella gave a joyous hoot and threw her arms around Jade. "Thank you, thank you, thank you! Maybe this will finally open his eyes to the fact that you're an exception to their stupid rule. An all-around exceptional woman that I am proud to call my friend!"

Jade's heart raced at the thought of being welcomed back into the Cassidys' inner circle. It was probably too soon to get her hopes up too high, but this was certainly a step in the right direction. "As your maid-of-honor, that technically puts me in charge of your bachelorette party and bridal shower." Ideas were already popping right and left as to what needed to be done next.

Bella pressed her hands over her mouth to cover another woot of exaltation. "Girl, I was only gunning for a cake and some flowers, but it will *not* break my heart if you throw a few parties into the mix. I don't know who will want to come, but…"

"How about we find out?" Jade raised her hand in a high-five, feeling more like her old self than she had in weeks. She represented one of the founding families of Chipper. There were ladies in town who would attend any event she threw together for that reason alone.

"Yes. Let's." Bella slapped her hand, dissolving into another round of joyous laughter.

CHAPTER 7: THE COMPETITION

BELDON

Two days later

BELDON'S HEART chilled with apprehension as he rode Sergeant across the grassy fields of Cassidy Ranch. His cell phone had been vibrating nonstop with incoming messages for the past thirty seconds or so. The last time that happened was when their oldest barn was on fire. Asher had been trapped inside, pinned beneath a beam.

Bringing his horse to a halt on a rocky incline overlooking the herd, Beldon reached around the rope coiled at his side to pull his cell phone from his back pocket.

It was a message thread his mother had started. *Family conference. Dinner at 7:00. All hands on deck, please.* She quickly added a second post. *No, I'm not referring to playing cards, Fox, though you're welcome to bring some.*

Beldon's shoulders relaxed at the realization that

there was no fire to put out this time. The responses his brothers were posting made him grin.

She's not referring to your boat, either. That was Asher.

Fox could always be counted on to add something pithy to the conversation. *How about I bring donuts? Beldon may not remember how to eat real food.*

And a horse. That was Devlin. *He eats most of his meals in the saddle.*

It was all too true. The only sit-down meals Beldon had enjoyed lately were their family lunches, which he only made it to about half the time. Oh, and the brisket dinner with the Arlettas last week. Rolling his eyes, he started typing. *Anything we should be worried about?*

Emerson responded first. *Besides your dining habits?*

Their mother sent a laughing face. Then she explained. *Need your input on a big decision concerning Chipper.*

Cormac finally popped into the thread. *Is this a black-tie affair?*

Fox zinged back a retort. *I'm still in bed. I'll be lucky if I can find a clean shirt.*

His mother issued a reprimand. *Shoes and shirts are NOT optional!*

Fox's next question was a single word. *Pants?*

Chuckling, Beldon pocketed his phone. Dinner at 7:00 meant he would not be making it to the Arlettas this evening, which was probably a good thing. It was Saturday, so there was a good chance that Jade and her friends would be home.

He hated the fact that a tall Navy SEAL was part of her current entourage. Jade had dragged him and his sister all over their small town, so the guy's name was common knowledge at this point — Todd Hoffman, a school superintendent from Dallas. He was college educated, in addition to being a veteran. If Beldon had been competing with the guy for Jade's attention, he wouldn't have stood a chance.

But I'm not. He had to keep reminding himself of that.

She'd been seen with Todd while touring the river, canyons, and Main Street shops. Rumors were now rolling faster than tumbleweeds about their budding romance. Folks were placing bets on how long it would take her to wheedle a proposal out of him. There was even a wager going about who would marry first, her or Asher.

Gritting his teeth, Beldon returned his attention to the cattle herd, trying not to dwell on his biggest fear — that he'd spent his entire adult life falling in love with the wrong woman. No matter how much he'd hoped and prayed about her over the years, it never seemed to lead to anything. The last kiss she'd given him had clearly been meant as a goodbye, and he was slowly coming to peace with that. He sure as heck would rather continue loving her from a distance for the rest of his days than to become the guy she simply killed time with between boyfriends.

A frenzy of barking alerted him to the fact that

there was trouble ahead. Pushing his worries about Jade aside, he lifted his reins and dug in his heels. "Come on, Sarge!"

The Mustang trotted forward a few feet, then came to a halt. Not more than twenty yards ahead of them, one of the new calves had gotten herself tangled in a patch of briars. Sharp thorns were scoring her flanks, drawing bright red trickles of blood. The pair of English sheepdog siblings who helped him herd the cattle were flanking the pitiful calf, preparing to face off with a trio of coyotes. The bristling creatures had crept beneath the wood slat fence and were slowly closing in on her from three directions.

"Easy, Sarge." Beldon silently willed the horse not to give into his fear and buck him off. They'd been through more than a dozen other hostile wildlife encounters together. However, each one was different.

He swiftly undid his saddle bag and pulled out a torch stick. Then he slid off the horse's back and jogged toward the bawling calf with the torch in one hand and his pistol in the other.

When the first coyote flicked a glance at him, he pushed the trigger on his torch. Orange flames shot out. The coyote yipped in alarm, spun away, and took off running. The second two coyotes continued their advance on the hapless calf. As Beldon drew closer, he could see white bubbles foaming from the wild creatures' muzzles. They were rabid, which meant their behavior would be unpredictable.

As the dogs kept up their frenzied barking, Beldon continued waving his flame torch, hoping to push the coyotes back a few feet. When they refused to budge, he knew he was going to have to risk a shot much closer to the calf than he would've liked.

Trying a different tactic, he stomped his boots and bellowed out a warning. The coyotes abruptly switched their attention to Beldon, stalking menacingly in his direction. Sarge gave a whinny of alarm behind him. Without warning, the coyotes leaped. Beldon fired two shots in quick succession. His bullets caught the rabid animals solidly in their chests. He still had to leap to one side as the yelping, flailing creatures sailed through the air and landed not too far from where he'd been standing. They writhed and whimpered on the ground for a few more seconds, then grew still.

Beldon put another bullet through each of them to ensure they didn't straggle back to their feet. Then he ran over to the wailing calf and dropped to his knees to unwind her from the briars. The moment she was free, she ran blubbering to her mother. Beldon returned to his saddle bag, grateful that Sarge had stood his ground like he'd been trained to do. Retrieving his medical kit, he jogged after the calf to swab her wounds with an antibiotic ointment. He would need to administer the treatment daily to ward off infection until the pesky little cuts scabbed over and healed.

Next, he disposed of the coyote carcasses, digging a shallow pit so he could burn them. Since they were rabid, he didn't want to take any chance of his cattle nosing through their remains and becoming infected.

The sun beat down hotter and hotter as the afternoon crept upon him. He guzzled down two water bottles in the space of an hour while continuously circling the herd to ensure no more coyotes were lurking. When he was satisfied that the danger was past, he retreated to the tree line to cool off.

His jeans were splattered with red from tending the injured calf. It was a good thing his mother's special meeting wasn't the black tie affair that Cormac had joked about, because there wasn't time for him to head home and change before dinner.

———

As Beldon drove up to his parents' ranch home, Asher pulled up behind him in his classic white Chevy. They parked on the side of the house where the gravel driveway forked off to the barns.

Beldon leaped down from his truck, dusting off his shirt and jeans as best he could. No doubt his appearance would draw some lively commentary from his brothers over dinner.

Asher strode around his truck, scowling in concern at the red spatter on his clothing. "Are you hurt?"

"Nope. We had a calf get caught in some briars."

"That's a lot of blood on your jeans." Asher's forehead remained wrinkled in concern.

"There was a trio of coyotes circling. Two were

rabid. Had to put them down. The third one ran off. Needless to say, the calf struggled long and hard to get away from them."

Asher hooked his thumbs through his belt loops, his scowl deepening. "Any reason you didn't call for backup?"

"Yeah, Mr. Ranch Manager. There was no time. It happened too fast."

"Understood." Asher whooshed out a breath. "Well, I'm glad you're okay. I have a change of clothes in my office, if you'd like to get cleaned up before dinner."

Beldon smirked. "Translated, you don't think it's wise for Mom to see me like this?"

There was an answering twitch to Asher's lips. "Something like that."

"Fine. You and I need to talk, anyway."

"So you said a few days ago." Asher fell into step beside him as they traversed the side lawn and headed toward the barn that served as their administrative office. "It's about Jade, if I correctly recall."

They entered the barn and clomped their way down the plank hallway leading to Asher's office.

"Yep." Beldon had never been one to beat around the bush. "I kissed her."

"Whoa!" Asher's boots churned to a halt at the door of his office. "You and Jade?" He threw an amazed look over his shoulder as he unlocked the door. "When?"

"The first time was right before you broke up. The second time was at the kissing booth at Chipper's

First Annual Hoedown. The third time was two days ago." Beldon knew his oldest brother would have questions, so he waited, wondering if they'd be throwing punches soon.

"Why'd you kiss her before we broke up?" Asher threw open the door and strode inside the office ahead of him. "Not that it makes any difference at this point, but that doesn't sound like you." He slapped at the wall, turning on the light switch.

"I didn't mean to." Beldon would never forget that fateful afternoon. He remembered every detail like it had just happened. "She was speeding down the main highway past our driveway. We almost had a head-on collision. When she pulled over to the side of the road, I ran over to check and make sure she was okay. She wasn't."

Asher yanked open a closet and produced the promised change of clothing, which he tossed to Beldon. "Was she hurt?"

Beldon caught the pile of clothing in mid-air and set it on the coffee bar by the door. "Not from our near collision, but she was pretty distraught. She was talking out of her head about being afraid that the next time you two broke up would be the last time. At one point, she babbled something about wishing I'd hit her with my truck and killed her. Guess I sort of snapped." He turned on the faucet by the coffee maker and leaned over the sink to wash the remaining bloodstains from his hands.

"And that's when you kissed her," Asher mused

in a voice infused with disbelief. "My monk of a younger brother."

"Yes. I'm sorry. It was wrong on every level. The moment she came to her senses, I told her it could never happen again. Then I drove away."

"Well, I'll be." Asher fell into the chair behind his desk, looking utterly stunned. "As far back as I can remember, you had a puppy dog crush on her. I never realized it ran any deeper than that."

"For what it's worth, I've regretted kissing her ever since," Beldon growled.

"Why?" Asher seemed more puzzled than angry.

"Because I'll never know how much my actions contributed to your breakup. I hope you can find it in yourself to forgive me someday, though I'll understand if you don't." Beldon unbuttoned his shirt and shrugged out of both it and the white undershirt he wore beneath it.

"There's nothing to forgive." Asher shook his head. "I should've cowboyed up and ended things with her months before the fire. I'm not sure why we dragged it out. I guess we'd been together for so long that it had become a habit. Everyone was expecting us to marry and…" He shook his head again.

Beldon was having a hard time connecting his brother's explanation to what happened next. "Then why were you so devastated when she broke up with you?" It made less sense than ever.

"Because I couldn't understand why she chose my discharge date from the hospital, of all times, to end things. I was weak and exhausted, with a ravaged face that was still healing. When my best friend in the world tucked tail and ran, I felt even more damaged — like I would never be whole again."

Devastated by the fire and the way she hurt your feelings, but not because your heart was broken? It took a moment for that to sink in. The guilt that Beldon had carried in his chest for so long started to ease. If everything Asher said was true, it was a game changer.

He bent over the sink again to splash water on his sweaty face. When he came up for air, he used his filthy shirt to wipe it dry. "I'm not sure the timing of her breakup had anything to do with you, bro."

"Why? What really happened between the two of you?" Asher straightened in his chair.

"Like I said, we kissed." Beldon wasn't sure what else his brother wanted to know.

"What did it feel like?"

Like my heart left my chest and settled in her hands. Beldon wasn't sure how to put it into words. "All I can tell you is, I felt something, and I've been feeling it ever since." He dragged his shirt over his face again.

"Well, that explains a lot!" Asher shot out of his chair and began to pace the floor behind his desk.

"If you say so. My brain feels like it's one big tangled roll of barbed wire." Beldon reached for the fresh shirt his brother had lent him.

"Because you're in love with her, you moron!"

Yeah. I know. Beldon's heart pounded faster as he

buttoned his shirt. "I'm a bloody range rider. Literally. She's a college graduate and a lawyer, to boot."

"So?"

"It would never work between us."

"How do you know if you haven't tried? Have you even told her that you love her yet?"

"What's the point?" Beldon fisted his hands at his sides. "In case you haven't noticed, she's with another guy now."

"She wasn't last month or the month before that. Why are you dawdling?"

Guilt. My own idiocy. Take your pick. "We've never dated each other's exes before," Beldon reminded, jaw tightening as they broached another tough subject.

"Holy cow, Beldon! Jade's not some dime-a-dozen ex." Asher rounded on him. "We've known her our entire lives. She's like family."

"She used to be," Beldon agreed wearily. He was pretty sure that ship had sailed. Jade all but hated him now.

"Shoot, Beldon! The whole reason we went gang busters on her after she broke up with me was because I thought she'd lost her mind. But if she did it because of what happened between the two of you, that changes things."

"How?" Beldon cried.

"For one thing, it was a pretty stinking honorable thing for her to do! Yeah, the timing with the fire was unfortunate, but she didn't two-time us. She made a clean break, and she's been groveling to get back into our good graces ever since."

"Jade? Groveling?" It wasn't a word Beldon would've ever used to describe her. The Jade Arletta he'd always known was too tough and sassy to grovel.

"Yes, groveling! In high style, of course, because it's Jade. Shoot, Beldon!" He rounded on his brother, eyes glowing with admiration. "She returned from Dallas last week with Bella's life savings in her hand and her teaching record expunged of all complaints."

"You have got to be kidding me!" Beldon's heart twisted painfully at how badly he'd misjudged her. "So that's why she flew to Dallas?" Not to go against his wishes by butting her nose into Bella and Asher's business, but because she still cared about their family. As mind-boggling as it was, it made sense.

"According to Bella, yes. They ran into each other by accident at a streetside cafe downtown. Bella said she was sipping tea by herself, pretty depressed about how unprepared she was to plan a wedding. When Jade showed up acting all concerned about finding her like that, Bella let it slip that she couldn't even afford a wedding dress. One thing led to another, and Jade ended up on a standby flight to Dallas the same afternoon."

"That sounds like Jade." Beldon snorted. "She's never been one to let grass grow under her feet."

"For which I am humbly grateful! After how hard we pushed her away, I'm flabbergasted she was still willing to put herself out there like that for us."

Because Jade has a mind of her own, that's why! A beautiful, intelligent, maddening one that Beldon knew he'd never fully figure out. He quickly ditched his filthy jeans and changed into the clean pair, tucking in his shirt before buttoning and zipping them. Then he buckled on his belt and stepped into his boots.

"So, when are you going to tell her how you feel?" Asher shot him a curious look as they headed back out the door.

"I'm pretty sure she already knows how I feel, but it doesn't matter. She's moved on." Beldon had spent the past year-and-a-half or so hating himself for cheating on his brother. Now he had a new reason to hate himself — for entirely misjudging Jade. It was no wonder she'd moved on. She deserved so much better than him.

"I'm not sure that's true. If you're still feeling the effects of your first kiss, that's not something you ever move on from. Trust me." Asher jammed his hands in his pockets as they trudged back towards the house. "I didn't think it was possible to care for someone as much as I care for Bella."

"Yeah, well, I'm pretty sure I blew it with Jade."

"Eh, give her some credit. She's made of tougher stuff."

"Either way, it's my problem. The only thing you need to do is keep loving Bella and focus on your wedding."

"I intend to, but this conversation isn't over."

"It is for now." Beldon snorted as they mounted

the porch steps. "Mom would skin us alive if we skipped her meeting." It didn't matter that all six of her sons towered over her these days. She was still a force to be reckoned with, and they adored her for it.

The moment they stepped inside the house, they were assailed with the mouth-watering scents of grilled meat and fresh-baked bread. Claire Cassidy presided over the feast, looking supremely contented like she always did when her entire brood was gathered. She waited until her hungry menfolk had packed away an entire tray of steaks before launching into her presentation.

"Buck Harrington has secured us a grant for the seed money to start our own school district," she announced, standing and waving her slender hands like she was unveiling something monumental, which she was.

Beldon watched her with interest. *A school district, eh?* He was proud of his mother for all of her moving and shaking.

"I'll let that sink in while I fetch our dessert." She left the room and returned, rolling her favorite wooden cart. It took a minute to hand out the plates of homemade cheesecake she'd prepared. Each slice was heaped with fresh picked berries from the raspberry patch out back.

"I already interviewed our first prospective superintendent," Claire Cassidy announced grandly as she returned to her seat.

Beldon and Asher exchanged a knowing glance. So that's why Todd Hoffman was in town.

"I take it we're referring to Jade's new boyfriend?" Beldon tried to sound casual.

His mother gave him a sharp look. "I do get the impression that's the direction Mr. Hoffman would like things to head. Despite the rumors flying around, though, I don't think they're officially dating."

"Yet," Fox added in a mocking voice.

"Is she the one who recruited the guy?" Beldon pressed, yearning to know exactly what he was up against.

"I didn't get that impression. He saw our advertisement online and asked her for more information about it while she happened to be in Dallas last week. I believe their connection is that they attended college together."

Asher waved two fingers in the air. "I can elaborate on their connection if you'd like."

"Please do." She reached for her husband's hand. He raised it to his mouth and pressed a tender kiss to it before lowering it to his knee.

"Jade flew to Dallas to face off with Bella's ex for the sole purpose of wrangling a settlement check out of him."

Mrs. Cassidy caught her breath. "Interesting! I had no idea Bella was her client."

"Not sure I would call it that. Seems that Jade and Bella have struck up a friendship, which they've been trying to keep quiet for all the obvious reasons."

"Awkward," Fox chortled beneath his breath.

Asher gave him a hard look. "Apparently, Jade

decided that getting back Bella's life savings was going to be her wedding gift to us."

Ridge Cassidy gave a long, low whistle. His dark eyes twinkled at his wife. "She's always been a pistol. Reminds me of another woman I know and love very much." He reached over to pinch her chin and give her a long, slow kiss in full view of his sons.

Fox made the obliging gagging sounds.

"Man! It's going to be really hard to keep giving Jade the stink eye going forward," Devlin mused. "What she did for Bella was huge."

"And Asher," Emerson cut in.

Fox waved his tea glass. "I hereby make a motion to issue her a full and immediate pardon for all past crimes. May her record forever be expunged!"

"Hear! Hear!" Devlin and Emerson crowed, raising their glasses.

"I never could work up the energy to hate her," Devlin added ruefully. "I'm kinda glad I don't have to keep faking it."

Beldon gazed around the table at the sentiments pouring out of his brothers, realizing he'd been the world's biggest fool not to bare his soul to Asher sooner.

As if on cue, Asher kicked him under the table. Leaning closer, he rasped in his ear, "She's all yours. Go get her, you dawg you!"

Their mother came up for air from the kiss their father had planted on her. Blushing, she reached over to tuck a strand of frosted hair behind his ear. "Getting back to the reason for our meeting," she announced breathlessly, "I'd like your honest opinion about hiring Todd Hoffman. I made a copy of his resume for each of you to review, and—"

"Please recuse me from the vote." Beldon scraped back his chair and stood. He was done dancing around the subject. "He seems like a decent guy, but I have a conflict of interest that'll be impossible for me to work around."

His mother's eyed widened in amazement. "Have you even met him in person?"

"Yes."

She looked bewildered. "When? I know he hasn't been in town for long."

"I was helping Luis with some chores the evening Jade returned to town with her guests in tow."

"Pardon the interrogation, but..." His mother blinked, as if trying to make sense of what he was saying. "Why in the world does Luis have you doing chores?"

"I offered."

"Doesn't he have ranch hands for that stuff?"

"He used to." Beldon shifted uncomfortably from one boot to the other. "I guess Jade never got around to telling you about her mother?"

Claire Cassidy shook her head, looking more concerned than ever. "Now that you mention it, I haven't seen Tandy in a while. I've been meaning to give her a call."

"Why don't you pay her a visit instead?" Beldon suggested quietly. "And don't tell her I sent you."

"What aren't you telling me, son?"

"It's not my news to share, Mom, but you need to go see her. Soon. That's all I'm at liberty to say."

"Oh, my lands!" she cried, shooting to her feet. "Our family meeting is adjourned. The rest of you boys need to review Todd's resume and get me an answer soon, you hear?"

"Yes, ma'am," they chorused.

She caught Beldon's eye again. "And I'd like a little more explanation about your recusal when I get back from checking on Tandy."

He gave her a two-fingered salute.

"Huh-uh! No way! I don't intend to spend another year of my life tiptoeing around the truth," Fox exploded, pushing back his chair. "So, here's the Cliff Notes version. Beldon has been in love with Jade since he was old enough to hold his first Crayon. The end."

A shocked silence met his announcement.

Devlin was the first to speak. "Oh, I see." He gleefully crossed his arms over his pressed white shirt. "You're recusing yourself from the vote, because Todd Hoffman is the competition."

Feeling his face turn red, Beldon pointed at the door. "I, ah, have a few things to take care of."

"Tell Jade I said hi," Fox sang out with a cocky tilt to his head.

Beldon wanted to sock him in the nose.

Instead of driving home as he'd originally planned, he found himself heading out to the main road. Almost of its own accord, his truck turned in the Arlettas' direction. It was just as well. Since his mother had opted to adjourn their family meeting early, there was no reason not to check in on Luis to see if he needed help with anything this evening.

He found his neighbor in the barn, brushing down a horse. It looked like he'd just returned from a ride. Standing beside him, brushing down a second horse, was none other than Todd Hoffman.

"Howdy, Beldon!" Luis called out cheerfully. "Didn't think you were going to make it this evening."

"We had a family meeting, but it ended early." Beldon glanced around. "What else needs to be done?"

"Nothing," Todd assured in a smooth voice. "We've already fed and watered the animals and gotten everything ready for tomorrow."

Beldon gave him a rigid nod. "Then I'll mosey on home." It looked like he'd wasted his time driving over here.

Luis tipped his hat at him. "Thanks for stopping by. I appreciate it."

"You bet." Beldon pivoted in his boots and strode from the barn, nearly plowing into Jade on his way back to his truck.

"Whoa, there!" Out of sheer habit, he reached out to steady her and didn't immediately drop his arms. He stood there, gazing helplessly down at her with his chest pounding from her nearness.

"Hi, Beldon." Her voice was thin and breathy.

He hardly recognized her with her hair pulled back in a ponytail and her long, slender legs encased in stone-washed jeans. For once, she was wearing regular boots. No high heels.

He gazed down at her with his heart in his eyes, longing to tell her how beautiful she was without her fancy suits and ridiculously high heels. Even more importantly, he wanted to tell her how much he loved her, but flowery words had never come easily to him.

When the pause in their conversation grew strained, she asked softly, "Did you ever get around to having that talk with Asher?"

"Yep. 'Bout an hour ago."

"Finally." Her cheeks paled a little. "What did he say?"

"That our rule about exes doesn't apply to you, because you're family." He knew he had no right to touch her, but he drew a calloused finger down her cheek. "That means your new boyfriend from Dallas is about to have some competition." They weren't flowery words, but they were straight from his heart.

Her lips parted on a gasp, but no words followed.

"From me," he added huskily, wanting to make his point clear. Afraid he'd do something stupid like kiss her again, he took a step back. This time, he intended to do things right by her. No more stolen kisses, crossed wires, or mixed signals. From now on, he was coming at her eyes wide open and speaking his mind.

It was hard letting go of her, though. He trailed his fingers down her arms, dragging out their parting as long as he could.

"Beldon," she breathed, tangling her fingers with his to keep him there a little longer. Her green gaze was beseeching, silently begging him to stay.

"I'll be back tomorrow, darlin'," he promised, "and the day after that and the day after that."

CHAPTER 8: BEST MAN WINS

JADE

June

JADE COULDN'T BELIEVE how quickly Bella and Asher's wedding rolled around. Between her new job with the Harrington law firm and managing her mother's ever-worsening condition, time had simply flown. The best part of her day was getting to see Beldon each evening. He never failed to show up. It was usually only for a few minutes, but it was a pleasant few minutes because they were no longer fighting.

It was progress. She still didn't feel like she had him back, though. Not completely. He was polite to her, but they didn't share the relaxed, easygoing banter of friends. They were more than that — he'd made that clear time and time again. But they were something that was impossible to define, since they weren't dating. He hadn't kissed her since their last argument, either, though he'd done an awful lot of kissing her with his eyes lately. It was about to drive her out of her mind!

As she stood in front of the mirror, she gave the sleeve of her lacy dress an agitated tweak, wondering if she'd ever understand the man. He cared for her. She was sure of it, but he wasn't doing anything about it. In fact, there were days she was worried he was only doing enough to keep her relationship with Todd from moving forward.

Todd had been doing a lot of traveling back and forth from Dallas lately. He had formally accepted the offer to serve as Chipper's first school superintendent and was tirelessly assisting Claire Cassidy and Buck Harrington to launch the district's infrastructure. No matter how busy he was, though, he never failed to squeeze in a visit with her over dinner.

It was as if both men in her life were waiting for her to make the next move — to decide between them.

"Is something wrong with your dress?" Bella joined her in front of the mirror, looking worried. They'd commandeered one of the Sunday School rooms adjacent to the foyer as the bridal dressing room.

"No. It's perfect." Unlike the many bridezillas who dressed their bridesmaids as horrible as possible, Bella had insisted that her maid-of-honor wear ivory lace and silk like herself. Jade's dress was cocktail length while Bella's was an off-the-shoulder ensemble that dragged the floor.

"Then why do you keep picking at it?" Bella stepped behind her to smooth her hands over the lacy cap sleeves.

"Because Beldon is about to see me in it." Jade still had no idea what he thought about her serving as Bella's maid of honor. As agreed, Asher had sprung the news on his brother last minute. "But that's my concern, not yours. The only thing you need to do today is be happy." She hated the fact that she'd allowed her nerves to show.

"Trust me. If I was any happier, I would explode." Bella's blue-gray eyes glowed. It wasn't often that her hair was unbraided, but she'd chosen to let the glossy, dark waves hang past her bare shoulders today. "I'm about to exchange vows with the man I love and start our happily-ever-after together. I'll belong to someone again and have a family again." Her eyes misted as she gently squeezed Jade's shoulders. "And none of it would have been possible without you."

"I can't take credit for that."

"Oh, but you can." Bella's forehead wrinkled with earnestness. "I've lost count of the number of couples I've met over the years who married because it was expected of them. Or because they were the right age and ready to start a family. Or, in some cases, for no other reason than they were afraid to be alone in the world. Not you, though." She shook her head, making her white gossamer veil dance back and forth.

"I've always marched to the tune of my own drummer," Jade said lightly, ready to change the subject. Bella was right, though. The whole town had expected her to marry Asher, and she'd very much hoped to start a family with him right up to the point when Beldon had kissed her. Her decision to end things with Asher and hold out for love had come at a bigger price than she'd anticipated, though. She'd been alone ever since. If she'd known how long she would remain single afterward, she might not have had the courage to do it.

"You are the strongest and kindest woman I know, Attorney Arletta." Bella adjusted a strand of Jade's hair and stepped back. "Which is exactly why I wanted you to wear bridal colors today. You deserve to be happy, too." She gave her a light nudge toward the door. "It's time. Go knock Beldon's socks off. Every instinct in me says he won't be able to resist you in this dress."

Jade was unable to say anything more past the lump in her throat. When she reached the door, however, she whirled around to give Bella one last hug.

They exchanged tremulous smiles. Then Jade turned the handle and stepped from the room. All the Cassidy brothers, except for Asher, were milling with their father in the roped off hallway outside the dressing room. They were busy checking cuff links and straightening bow ties.

At the sight of Jade, they paused their grooming, eyes widening in admiration.

"Wow!" Fox swaggered her way first. "I thought

Bella was the one getting married." He looked positively princely in his silver, long-tailed tuxedo jacket as he pulled out his cell phone and pretended to check his calendar. "Yep. She's the one."

"Move over, goofball." Beldon appeared in front of her. Like an eclipse, his broad shoulders blocked everyone else from view. "He's right about the wow part."

"Thank you." She drank in his dark good looks. "I haven't seen you in a tux since our high school prom." He'd attended it, but he hadn't brought a date. As far as she knew, she was the only one he'd asked out, and she'd turned him down in lieu of going with Asher.

"Maybe because they're so blasted comfortable," he returned dryly. "I feel like I'm choking in this bowtie."

"You look fabulous." Without thinking, she reached up to loosen it. "I'm sorry." She hastily dropped her hands. "I shouldn't have done that."

"Why not?" His voice was husky.

She lowered her voice so that only he could hear her. "I know we're not exactly friends anymore."

"Good, because I never wanted to be your friend." His blue gaze glinted into hers. "I've always wanted more."

"Beldon." Her breath came out in a helpless whoosh. "We can't do this here." She blushed at the thought that someone might overhear them.

"I wasn't planning on it." He stepped closer,

gazing at her with undeniable longing. "After the wedding, though, all bets are off."

She caught her breath at the look in his eyes. "What do you mean?"

"Watching my brother tie the knot today will be 100% proof I didn't personally destroy his happiness. Guess it's my own version of The Rule."

"Beldon Cassidy," she murmured shakily, "you are, without a doubt—"

She was unable to finish as he swooped closer to speak directly in her ear. "Crazy about you?"

Her eyelashes fluttered against her cheeks.

"Insanely jealous of Todd?" he added silkily.

"We are not an item," she declared breathlessly. "I don't know why you keep insisting that we are."

"He wants to be."

She lifted her chin. "At least he's not afraid to tell me how he feels."

Beldon's blue eyes flamed dangerously. "Has he told you he loves you?"

"No. Neither have you."

"Yet you've always known it."

She felt close to swooning. It was so unfair of him to do this now! "Beldon," she glanced dizzily around them, "it's time to—"

"Walk down the aisle, I know."

She felt like laughing and crying at the same time as he offered his arm to her. When she tucked her hand around it, he covered it with his other one and gazed at their joined hands in satisfaction.

"I finally have you exactly where you belong, Jade Arletta." His voice was gravelly with emotion.

She caught her breath, wishing they were alone — dying to be alone with this new and brazen version of him!

The next forty-five minutes passed in a swirl of emotions that she couldn't begin to sort out. Beldon's steely bicep beneath her trembling fingers was the only thing that kept her upright on their promenade down the aisle. The church was crammed full of people.

Her knees grew weak all over again when they reached the altar. Instead of allowing her to slip her hand back to her side, he lifted it to his mouth and pressed a kiss to her knuckles just like she'd seen his father do to his mother's hands countless times.

She felt painfully bereft when they parted ways to stand on opposite sides of the rose trellis where the minister was waiting. Within minutes, Asher and Bella sealed their vows by exchanging white gold rings. Hers sported a square-cut diamond that flashed beneath the sunlight pouring through the stained glass windows on either side of the sanctuary.

At the conclusion of the ceremony, Beldon moved back to the center of the aisle and beckoned for Jade to join him. She felt like she was floating on a cloud toward him.

He bent to speak one word in her ear on their walk back up the aisle. "Mine." Her heart raced with anticipation.

Though she'd ridden with her parents and Todd to the wedding, Beldon towed her toward his truck in the parking lot.

"I should let my family know where I'm at," she informed him breathlessly. It didn't feel right to mention Todd.

"I already told your dad."

"Really? When?" She didn't see how it was possible.

"Yesterday." He led her to the driver's side of his truck and gently lifted her inside. Leaping up beside her, he hooked an arm around her shoulders. "Unless you tell me no, I'm about to kiss you, and I don't know when I'm going to stop."

She wordlessly tipped her face up to his.

He brushed his mouth across hers, taking his time and savoring each sigh he drew from her. She had to wrap her arms around his neck and hold on as the storm overtook them.

By the time he lifted his head, the parking lot was empty.

She pressed her palm in wonder to his cheek, adoring the rough drag of his jaw against the pads of her fingers. Though he'd shaved this morning, his evening shadow was showing up early. "You're right," she whispered. "I don't think we can be friends."

He turned his face to drop a lingering kiss on her palm. "Years ago, I asked you out on a date, and you told me no. If I ask you the same question again, will you give me a different answer?"

"Yes." Happy tears stung the backs of her eyelids. If she'd been a smarter girl, she would have given him a different answer back then.

"Will you be my girl, Jade?"

"I will." From inside her beaded handbag, her phone buzzed with an incoming call.

"All of me for all of you. No sharing. I can't do this any other way."

Her heart raced at his boldness. He wanted to be exclusive from the get-go, and she was very much okay with that. "I don't want to share you, either."

Her phone continued to buzz as they gazed in wonder at each other.

"I should probably get that," she murmured.

"Okay." He kept his fingers on the back of her neck, drawing gentle swirls there.

It was Todd. He sounded worried. "Where are you?"

"With Beldon."

"Are you alright?" he asked quickly.

"Yes." She dreamily gazed up at Beldon, tracing his strong nose and hard jaw with her eyes.

"Are you going to make it to the reception?"

"Of course! We'll be there..." she looked at Beldon for confirmation, "soon."

He reached up to disconnect the phone before she could say anything else. "Now where were we?" Tipping up her chin, he leaned in for another tender kiss that left her dizzy.

His phone buzzed next. This time, it was Asher.

Beldon tapped a button to put him on speaker phone. "Everything okay, bro?"

"Not really. I seem to be missing my best man. Any idea when he's going to show up?"

"I'm on my way," Beldon assured, waggling his dark eyebrows at Jade.

She dissolved into silent laughter, hoping he didn't divulge what he'd been up to for the past half hour.

"Where are you?"

"In the church parking lot."

"What? Never mind. Listen, if the church is still unlocked, I need a favor."

"Listening."

"Bella left her bridal bouquet in the dressing room."

"I'll grab it. Anything else?"

"Yeah. Get here!"

———

Jade arrived at the wedding reception with Bella's bouquet in her hands and Beldon's arm slung possessively around her shoulders. The double doors of the Cassidy's store were flung wide, and the inside had been transformed into a banquet hall. The shelves had been pushed back to make room for more than a dozen round tables draped in white linen.

Under Jade's oversight, the local florist had artfully strung green vines and white lights around the ceiling. The piece de resistance, however, was the wedding cake tower. It was crafted from three tiers of pine log platters. On the lower two tiers were alternating vanilla and chocolate cupcakes. On the top tier was a small wedding cake bearing a cowboy and cowgirl topper.

Bella had begged her to keep things simple, so Jade had. The room was overflowing with laughter, happy chatter, and the smiles of friends and family. The refreshments were arrayed in a buffet line against the wall, manned by Cormac, Devlin, Emerson, and Fox. They'd removed their tuxedo jackets and had rolled up the sleeves of their white dress shirts. They were still killing it in their gray trousers and black cowboy boots, though.

Bella glided their way on Asher's arm, laughing at something he said.

Jade tried to hand over the bouquet, but the happy bride waved it away. "It's yours, my friend. I was going to throw it straight to you, anyway."

Asher eyed the arm Beldon had around Jade's shoulders with such intense curiosity that she blushed. He winked at her. "Since you two are running so late, Bells and I decided to start the dancing. We'll circle back to the toasts later."

Beldon didn't look the least bit apologetic. "I had my reasons." He bent to nuzzle Jade's earlobe. "Very. Good. Reasons."

His parents approached them. To be more precise, his mother towed his father in their direction. Her blonde hair was piled high and held in place with a white rose clip. "We've been looking all over for you, son!" Though her glance at Jade was infused with curiosity, she merely added, "You did an amazing job with the decorations, Jade. You really outdid yourself this time." It was unclear if she was still speaking about the candle and rose vine centerpieces or the happiness glowing from her second oldest son's eyes.

All Ridge did was crinkle his eyes at her, but Jade could have wept with joy from the warm acceptance she read in his gaze.

"Thank you, Claire," she murmured, feeling her lashes grow damp.

As the music started, Ridge spun his wife away and Beldon turned Jade back toward him, cuddling her close. She wrapped her arms around his neck, allowing the bouquet to drape down his back.

"I love you, Jade."

Her lips parted in wonder. It was the first time he'd ever said the words out loud to her. Before she could find her voice, Todd cut in on their dance.

"May I?" He raked Beldon with a dark, hooded look.

"Only if you keep it short." Beldon took a step back, brazenly caressing her with his eyes.

Todd sashayed her away from him. "You want to tell me what's going on?"

"Beldon finally asked me to date him, and I said yes."

"That happened rather suddenly."

"Actually, it's been a long time coming." It had been years in the making.

"Are you happy?" He studied her with concern.

"Never mind. That's a dumb question. I've never seen you like this before, not even when you were dating Asher."

"Thank you for understanding." She hoped she hadn't hurt his beautiful heart too much with her choice, because she knew she'd made the right one. There was someone else out there for him. There had to be. He was simply too amazing to remain single for much longer.

"So long as you're happy, then I'm happy for you. Not too happy for myself, at the moment, but..." He gave her a lopsided grin.

Beldon cut back in a few seconds later. "Did you tell him?"

"I did."

"He didn't seem too broken up about it."

"We weren't dating." She gave the hair behind his neck a light yank. "Something tells me you went out of your way to make sure we didn't."

"I was keeping your options open, darlin'." He dipped his head to brush her lips tenderly with his. "In case you decided not to make a go of it with your tall, educated, and refined superintendent friend, I wanted you to know there was a dusty range rider waiting on the sidelines."

"You were never on the sidelines." She twined her arms around his neck again. "You were constantly helping out my father and looking in on my mother. And somewhere along the way, you completely and irrevocably lassoed my heart, cowboy."

"Are you sure my lack of a college education isn't going to be a problem for us?"

"Oh, my!" Her eyes widened teasingly. "Is the fearless Beldon Cassidy actually afraid of something?"

"Only of losing you, darlin'."

"You do realize that I'm in love with you?"

"Are you?" His piercing gaze softened. "It's the first time you've said it."

"It's the first time I've been in love," she confessed softly.

"I like the sound of that."

The dance came to an end, and someone called for a toast. Beldon kept his short and sweet. "To love." He raised his tea glass. "The greatest gift of all." He met and held Jade's gaze as he spoke.

It was a reference to her favorite verse in the Bible, and a wedding reception was the perfect time to quote it.

"To love," the gathering of family and friends chorused.

"To love," Jade echoed, raising her glass of lemon water.

Before the evening was over, she overheard numerous complaints about how "that Arletta girl" had "already nabbed herself another Cassidy." One woman went as far as to say, "You'd think by now they'd see through her games."

Their predictions were equally cutting.

"It won't last long."

"She'll drop him like a hot potato when she grows tired of him."

"That sweet boy is about to have his heart trampled."

Jade lifted her chin and pretended she didn't hear them.

CHAPTER 9: MESSAGE IN SMOKE

BELDON

July

SOME DAYS BELDON saw so little of Jade that they might as well have been dating long distance. He worked from dawn until dusk, and her new job was ruthlessly demanding, often requiring her to slog through paperwork long into the evening after she returned home. He wracked his brain for ways to carve out more time with her and came up with only one. Though they hadn't been dating long, he was going to have to convince her to marry him soon.

It took him a full day in the saddle to come up with his game plan. Then it took another month to get all the pieces in place to host a rodeo down at the fairgrounds. It ended up being easier than expected to keep his plans to propose to Jade a secret, because she assumed he was simply organizing another charity event, this time for the new school district under construction.

The night before the rodeo, he knocked on the front door of her home, shifting from one boot to the other while he waited. Because of the text messages they'd been trading, he knew she was still working on a case file and hated to interrupt. However, he couldn't bear to let a single day go by without telling her that he loved her.

Jade pushed the door open for him, looking exhausted.

"I'm not coming in, because I know you're busy." He didn't have the heart to ask her to step outside. "I just came to tell you I love you before I head home." He'd helped her father feed and water his herd, as well as perform a minor repair on one of the tractors. They were planning on cutting hay over the weekend.

Her exhaustion faded a few degrees as a dreamy look crept into her eyes. "Most guys would've just texted that."

"You can't see how I really feel when I say it over the phone."

"I love you, too, Beldon. So much!" She pushed the door wider and stepped outside to join him on the porch, pulling it shut behind her.

He whistled in admiration at the cut-off jean shorts encasing her tanned legs. "You just set off a five-alarm fire inside me, darlin'." Though he knew she needed to get back to work, he couldn't resist leaning in for a kiss. Man, but he'd missed her today! He resisted the urge to take her in his arms, knowing he reeked of hay, tractor oil, and sweat.

She closed the distance between them to wind her arms around his neck. "If you're going to knock on my door and interrupt my work, cowboy, you'd better do it right."

His arms banded around her, tugging her flush against him. "Sorry about the stench."

"I grew up on a farm, remember?"

"Thanks, I think." He buried his face against the side of her neck, soaking in her sweetness. "Still can't believe you're mine." It blew his mind that his hotshot attorney girlfriend had agreed to date a lowly range rider. "I thank God every day for you, babe."

She gave a soft, sighing laugh. "That's so much nicer than what the rest of Chipper has to say about me these days."

He knew what she was talking about and wished there was a way to shield her from the gossip. All he could do, though, was wait and hope the locals would find something else to talk about soon, rather than his number one gal. "They don't know you like I do." He stroked a hand through her long, glossy hair.

She tipped her head back to gaze up at him. "Just for the record, your opinion matters more to me than all of them put together."

He palmed her cheek. "You're one heck of a lawyer. You'll win them over one case at a time."

She made a pouty face at him that made him want to kiss her senseless. "My newest client this morning swore the only reason she came to me was because of my cut-throat reputation."

He was unable to hold back a guffaw. "So long as you keep swinging your sword at their dragons, darlin', they'll keep coming to you." He couldn't have been more proud of the work she was doing in their community, even taking a pro bono case here and there on the sly when a client couldn't afford to pay.

"Thank you, Beldon. I needed to hear that tonight." She stretched on her bare tiptoes to give him a lingering kiss that left them both breathing unevenly. "Alright. If I'm going to help you run the press box at the rodeo tomorrow, I really do have to get more work done tonight. I wish I didn't. When you hold me like this, I don't ever want to leave your arms."

"Right back atcha, darlin'." Her words made Beldon more hopeful than ever of receiving a positive answer to the all-important question he planned to ask her tomorrow. "Just so you know, I love you more today than I did yesterday." He brushed his thumb over her lower lip. "And I'm going to love you even more tomorrow, you hear?"

"Tomorrow suddenly seems too far away." It was with great reluctance that she slipped from his embrace.

It was for him, too, but he knew she wasn't exaggerating the amount of paperwork she had left to finish tonight. "I'll pick you up at eight."

She blew him a kiss. "Hurry up, tomorrow!"

———

Jade was taken aback to wake up and find her parents getting ready to depart the house. At first, she feared her mother had taken a turn for the worse during the night, but Tandy Arletta vehemently denied it.

"I know it doesn't seem possible, given my last medical report, but I actually feel better this morning than I have in days." She was sporting a new chin-length bob with stacked layers in the back, claiming it felt lighter and cooler than her longer hair. Jade knew the real reason she'd cut it, though, was because she didn't have the energy left to style it most days.

"We're not leaving quite as early as you, though," her mother continued in the same cheerful voice.

"Are you sure you want to deal with the noise and commotion of a rodeo? Not to mention the heat? It's supposed to be hot today." Jade worriedly checked the weather app on her cell phone and winced at the forecast. The forecast was predicting it would reach 101 degrees by mid-afternoon.

Her mother didn't look even a tad discouraged. "Beldon said he'd make sure we had seats on the shaded side of the arena. Plus, he's getting us tickets to the clubhouse level. If it gets too hot, we can watch from the windows in an air conditioned room. Worse case scenario, your dad will bring me home early."

Jade gave up arguing and sent her a thumbs up. "It

sounds like you have solid plans A, B, and C in place." Far be it from her to tell an aging former barrel racer that she couldn't attend a rodeo. Since her mother would be arriving at the fairgrounds in a wheelchair, Jade additionally deduced she was finally ready to go public with the news of her diagnosis. *Go get 'em, Mom!*

As promised, Beldon's truck rumbled up the driveway at the crack of 8:00. His Stetson was pushed back and his sleeves rolled up as he hopped down to assist her into the truck.

"I can't believe my parents are coming to the rodeo," she breathed by way of a greeting, wondering how long he'd known about it.

"I can. Luis mentioned something about your mom being anxious to get out of the house." He joined her in the seat and scooted closer to slant his mouth over hers. "Morning," he muttered when he lifted his head. "You look rested."

"So do you." She touched his cheek. "Did you dream of me?"

"Always." He kissed her again before revving the motor and taking off.

The number of trucks and horse trailers piling into the parking lot of the fairgrounds was truly astonishing.

"Did you invite everyone in the state?" Jade gazed out the window, watching all the gorgeous horses being unloaded and saddled.

"Pretty much." He eyed the fast-filling parking lot. "With only a month of prep time, I had to spread the word far and wide to guarantee we'd have enough participation."

He elaborated on that point during his opening remarks as the rodeo's master of ceremonies. She remained in the press box while he stood in the arena with a microphone in his hand, addressing the crowd that was jammed into the bleachers.

"I want to thank you folks for coming out today in support of our charity rodeo. Today's proceeds are going to a worthy cause — our very own Chipper School District!" He paused while they clapped and cheered. "Something we didn't announce in advance is another very special event taking place today, because we wanted to keep it a secret as long as we could. Many of you have probably already noticed the silent auction taking place on the sidewalk by the concession stand. All the proceeds from our silent auction will go to a beloved member of our community, and here she is."

Jade gaped as her father stepped through a side gate to roll her mother's wheelchair to the center of the arena. A ripple of gasps worked its way across the audience as it dawned on them who they were looking at.

"Tandy Arletta," Beldon continued warmly, "is one of Chipper's unsung heroes. She doesn't say much, but you can always count on her to show up when you need an extra set of hands at the soup kitchen, the holiday clothing drives, or the ticket table at our first annual hoedown last summer. And after giving so much of her time and herself to all of us, she could use a little giving in return. I have her permission to share that she was recently diagnosed with Multiple Sclerosis."

A sigh of regret rose from his listeners.

"She needs a miracle, folks. And while her loved ones are praying for that miracle, we're going to surround her with an extra dose of love, concern, and generosity today. The money you spend at the silent auction will go towards some much-needed services like housecleaning and meal deliveries."

Tears trickled down Jade's face at the planning and effort he must have put into the silent auction. She listened as he went on to describe the many donations to the cause — right down to the baskets of wild honey personal indulgence products from Cassidy Farm.

The barrel racing event began right after his introductory remarks. It was followed by the bronc riding competition. Fox won yet another buckle to add to his growing collection.

Jade couldn't believe how long her parents stayed and watched the events. Her mom had to be getting tired, but she was constantly surrounded by friends, which had to be a wonderful feeling.

After the calf roping event, Beldon took the field again with his microphone in hand. "There's another very special citizen I'd like to honor today. Some of you only know Jade Arletta by her runway looks and the ridiculously high heels she insists on wearing for reasons I will never understand."

His words were met with chuckles. "Others of

you know her from the many events she's helped coordinate around town over the years, to include this one. I think we can all agree that if there's any big project needing to be planned and organized to perfection — Jade is the person to call."

There was a smatter of clapping that he talked right through. "And now that she's joined the Harrington law firm, even more of you are calling her, because she's proven time and time again that she has what it takes to face and slay our dragons." He paused a moment. "Legally speaking, that is. I know of one boy in town who wishes I was referring to real, fire-breathing dragons. Sorry, kid."

More laughter erupted. "There's one more thing you need to understand about Jade Arletta. I love her."

She caught her breath. *Oh, Beldon!* She hadn't been expecting any of this.

He pivoted to the press stand to meet her gaze. "I've loved her for as long as I can remember — all the way back to when we were playing tag and hide-and-go-seek together."

His listeners peppered the air with aw's.

"I asked her to be my girl not too long ago, and she said yes. Well, today I have another question to ask her."

Oh, my goodness! Jade pressed a hand to her heart, reminding herself to breathe. Though Beldon stopped talking, he continued to hold her gaze while her insides degenerated into an agonized snarl of anticipation. He seemed to be waiting for something.

For a moment, silence blanketed the arena. Then her ears picked up the distant drone of an airplane engine. As the engine grew louder, Beldon angled his head upward, coaxing her to follow the sound with her gaze.

She looked up to see the Cassidys' red crop duster fly into view overhead. The pilot took a sharp dive at an angle that made the audience yelp in alarm and shoot to their feet. Then a puff of thick white smoke appeared. The plane circled around and did another dive, forming the other side of a V with his next puff of smoke. Two dives later, the V had turned into a W. It took three more dives and four more puffs of smoke to turn the W into a word — Will.

Both of Jade's hands were pressed to her chest now, realizing that Beldon was asking her a question. A very important, earth-shaking one that it took the airplane several more dives and loops to finish. In the end, the words *Will You Marry Me* were painted in white smoke across the blue Texas sky. The W and next few letters were quickly dissipating in the morning breeze.

Someone tried to press a microphone into Jade's hands, but she pushed it away. Beldon's hopeful smile slipped. Heart pounding, she reached blindly for the railing and moved down the small flight of steps. When her feet reached the dirt floor of the arena, she broke into a run.

The rest of the world dimmed as she ran toward the one man in the world who'd become everything to her — a man who'd refused to be her friend while continuing to be the best neighbor in the universe to her parents, a man who'd always been there when she needed him the most, a man who'd loved her long before she knew it and better than she deserved.

"Yes!" she cried shakily as she reached him.

His arms were already outstretched. Since the microphone was still in his hand, it caught her breathy answer. She leaped into his arms, and he spun her around and around. He briefly shouted into the mike, "She said yes, folks!" Then he dropped it to the ground and claimed her lips.

The cheering and applause were deafening. Happy tears were streaking down Jade's cheeks by the time Beldon set her feet back on the ground. Then he produced a small black felt box.

The microphone was still on the ground. His words were for her alone. "For years, my oldest brother swore he would never marry. So to be safe, my great-grandparents willed this ring to me instead. Will you wear it for me?"

Her eyed widened in amazement at the gorgeous oval diamond surrounded by tiny diamonds, knowing it probably cost more than he made in a year. It seriously looked like it belonged in a museum.

"You know I will." She held out her hand.

He slid the ring on her finger and drew her back into his arms. "I wasn't sure this day would ever come, but you're finally with the right Cassidy brother."

"I am." She cupped his face in her hands, feeling

like she'd just been handed the world. Never before had she felt so loved, cherished, and safe.

"One more thing, darlin'," he added huskily, "I've waited years for this moment, so I'm not gunning for a long engagement."

A wave of happiness swept through her — one that left her so dizzy that it was a good thing he was still holding on to her. "I don't want a long engagement, either." She wasn't sure how much time her mother had left and wanted her to be there for their special day.

Most of all, Jade was ready for all of her to belong to all of him.

———

Cormac banked the plane left and circled the arena one last time, leaving a wide ring of smoke puffs that resembled popcorn. There were two big charity events going on down below today. He wanted to do his part to keep the crowd happy and in a generous mood.

Fox's voice crackled across his radio. "In case you're wondering, farm boy, Beldon's lady said yes."

"Roger that. Heading back to home base."

There was no airport or air traffic control tower in the tiny town of Chipper, so the Cassidys had built their own version of one for their crop duster jet. It consisted of a single-lane landing strip in the back field with a tower not much bigger than a deer stand. So far, Cormac was the only brother who'd earned his pilot's license, but Fox was toying with the idea of getting his. Cormac hoped his thrill seeking youngest sibling followed through, because he could really use some help with the task.

"The runway is clear for landing," Fox announced.

"Roger. Roger." Cormac never took off or landed without a family member in the tower to keep a lookout for hazards in the air or on the ground.

He and Fox were soon rumbling back toward the arena in Fox's juiced-up off-roading vehicle. It was an open top rig complete with roll bars. Their mother called it "a big toy for a big boy," since Fox was forever horsing around with it on the ranch — driving donuts in the fields and stirring up dust clouds.

"So, Beldon's engaged." Fox shot him a devilish grin from behind the steering wheel.

"Yep." Cormac was happy for Beldon. He found it kind of humorous that the guy who'd ultimately put a ring on the classy Jade Arletta was the only Cassidy brother who hadn't gone to college. Even Fox was taking online classes in and around his rodeo schedule. Guess there was some truth to the old saying that opposites attract.

"Guess that means you're next." Fox shot him another grin.

Cormac was only half listening to him, so it took an extra second to register what he'd said. "Wait! What?"

"Brother number two will be hitched soon, which

means Mom will start dangling single ladies in front of you next."

"Then she'll be wasting her time. There's not a woman in this town who revs my motor that way." He wasn't speaking off the cuff. It was a small town, and he'd met everyone in it. "Besides, there's no law that says I have to be next."

"Nope, but Claire Cassidy is a law unto herself, and she wants grandkids."

"Then Asher and Bella had better get busy, because I don't have so much as a single prospect lined up."

"Dude! You're about to turn twenty-eight. If you need me to give you some pointers with the ladies—"

"No, I do not need any pointers from my renegade youngest sibling, thank you."

"Hey, you're the one moaning about your lack of prospects, bro."

"I wasn't moaning. Just stating facts."

"It sounded like moaning."

"That was just the wind in your ears, moron." As Fox steered into the arena parking lot and slowed, Cormac leaped out while it was still moving.

Fox skidded to a halt beside him. "Yo! You tired of my company or something?"

"What gave you that idea?" Cormac kept walking.

"Just a word of warning, farm boy." Fox rolled his off-roader alongside Cormac, keeping pace with him. "One of Mom's biggest tricks seems to be asking one of us to give so-and-so a ride home. It sounds like an

179

innocent request, but it's not. All of her so-and-sos are single and beautiful, and it generally means she's got her next daughter-in-law picked out, so you'd better run."

It sounded so much like their mother that Cormac snorted out a laugh. "Why are you telling me this?"

"To save you from disaster, so you'll owe me a favor."

"What do you want, Fox?" Cormac had no interest in playing games.

"Flying lessons."

"You could've just asked."

"Nah! It'll be more fun hearing you say I was right."

Shaking his head, Cormac made his way toward the arena. Behind him, Fox hit the gas pedal and roared off in a squeal of rubber against the pavement.

The town of Chipper was lucky to have an event center at all, particularly one this size. The enormous white pole barn wasn't fancy, but it was sturdy and could hold an entire rodeo, plus all the fairs, carnivals, and 4-H events their town was quickly growing famous for.

Stepping through the turnstile entrance gate, he waved his season pass at the grandmotherly woman collecting tickets.

"Oh, hi Cormac! Nice flying up there today."

"Thank you, ma'am. I—"

"Sweetheart! There you are," his mother sang out, sashaying his way in her jeans and sassy red boots. "I've been looking high and low for you. Well, mostly high." She chuckled and pushed back her straw hat to gaze affectionately up at him. "That was some stunt you pulled for Beldon!"

"I heard she said yes, so I'm gonna call it a win." He leaned closer to envelope her in a bear hug.

"Oh, Cormac!" she sighed, hugging him back. "I'm about to have another son married. I'm so happy I could pop."

"Glad I could help." He kissed her cheek. *Not interested in being next.*

"Speaking of helping… Oh, sheesh! I almost forgot." She pulled away from him, glanced frantically around the entry area.

"What's wrong, Mom?" Cormac followed her gaze.

"I need a favor, hon." She dropped her voice. "Remember that superintendent friend of Jade's?"

"Yep."

"Well, he brought his sister back into town so they can do some house shopping together. Long story short, her son has asthma, and they forgot to bring his inhaler."

"Sorry to hear it." Cormac wasn't sure what any of this had to do with him.

"I know you just got here, but she needs a ride back to the Arlettas' place, and I'm having trouble finding anyone else to do it. Mr. Harrington has her brother in a closed-door meeting, and I couldn't possibly ask Luis to leave Tandy's side — that poor woman! — not even for a few minutes."

It was all Cormac could do not to laugh out loud.

It looked like he'd be owing Fox some flying lessons soon. "Sorry, Mom." He kept his voice bland. "I didn't drive here, so I don't have any wheels…" His voice died as a young woman with a long, dark ponytail stepped away from the bleachers, holding a little boy's arms over his head.

Her curvy frame was encased in jeans and a filmy red shirt that left her shoulders bare. A camouflage backpack was slung over one arm with a kid's water bottle peeping out from the side of it. One hundred percent of her attention was on her kid. Her body practically vibrated with motherly concern as she led him toward the exit gate.

Whoa! She was seriously hot. He wondered where her husband was, the lucky dog. A quick glance around proved that she was alone, and that's when he realized this must be the woman his mother wanted him to give a lift.

The boy made a choking sound that caused his mother's face to turn pale. At first, he'd assumed they were playing a game. He'd been wrong. The kid was clearly in the throes of an asthma attack. Cormac recognized the signs.

His protective instincts kicked in. Jogging toward the ticket booth, he snatched up a chair. "Sorry. Need to borrow this real quick. I'll bring it back." Then he jogged toward the mother and son to drop the chair beside the boy. He took a knee in front of him.

"Hey! My name is Cormac, and I'm going to help you, okay?"

The boy nodded, coughing and looking alarmed.

His dark curly hair was sticking out in all directions from beneath the brim of a red and blue baseball cap.

Cormac had been through similar situations before on the baseball field, so he knew what to do. "Listen, I'm going to have you take a seat, and we're going to play a little game together."

He motioned for the kid's mother to assist him. "Unbutton his jeans for me, will ya?" He wanted to remove as many restrictions as possible to the boy's air flow.

As soon as he was seated, Cormac started speaking again. "Okay. We're going to breathe in through our noses and push the air out of our mouths. Can you do that?"

The boy nodded, still coughing.

"Alright, let's go. Breath in." Cormac waved his hands in an upward movement toward his own chest, taking in a large mouthful of air. He made sure it was enough to make his cheeks poke out like a chipmunk. "Now breathe out." He slowly whooshed out his breath. "Breath in again."

Each time Cormac took another breath, he made silly faces like he was a balloon about to pop. Each time he breathed out, he made snoring sounds or pretended to be a train whistle.

In no time, the kid was so focused on his antics that he started to smile. Once his fear was under control, his shoulders relaxed and his breathing became easier.

They continued to play Cormac's "game" for the

next several minutes until he was certain the danger was past.

At one point, Cormac had the kid giggling so hard that he reached over and rubbed his knuckles across his baseball cap. "Easy there, tiger." He didn't want to incite another asthma attack.

"Are you a clown?" the kid snickered.

"Actually, I'm a Little League coach. Do you play baseball?"

He nodded excitedly. "I'm our first baseman."

"That's an important position." Cormac gave him a high-five and finally glanced over at his mother.

Her dark eyes were shining with gratitude. The sheen of dampness covering them told him that she'd been truly worried about her son's condition.

"Hi." He stood and thrust out a hand. "Cormac Cassidy. Farmer by day and Little League coach by night."

When she slipped a delicate hand in his, he noted her fingernails were lacquered in patriotic red, white, and blue colors — probably for the 4th of July celebrations that would be taking place tomorrow.

"Ellie Roberts. Kindergarten school teacher and mother of this six-year-old rascal."

He squeezed her fingers, in no hurry to let her hand go, though he did. When she reached up to hitch the camouflage backpack higher on her shoulder, he noted she wasn't wearing a wedding ring.

"And I'm Jackson," her son announced proudly, springing out of the chair like a jackrabbit and giving a little hop as he buttoned his britches.

Cormac rubbed his knuckles over the top of his ball cap again. "I hear we need to head back to the ranch to lasso us an inhaler."

"Yes, sir!"

"You're gonna have to help your mama remember it in the future, you hear?"

"Yes, sir!"

Cormac felt the scrape of keys against his palm as his mother slid her keychain into his hand from behind. "Take my truck, hon. I'm parked on the east side of the arena. I'll return the chair to the ticket booth for you." She stepped around him to retrieve the chair Jackson had vacated.

"Thanks." He closed his fingers around the keys, realizing he'd just been outmaneuvered by his matchmaking mama. There was no ensuing swell of irritation, though. The thought of driving the lovely Ellie Roberts and her cute-as-a-peanut son home didn't feel like too terrible of an inconvenience.

Especially when she made no attempt to flirt with him. If anything, she seemed to withdraw the moment he helped her and Jackson climb into the cab of his mother's shiny red pickup truck.

The only sound when Cormac joined them behind the wheel was the cell phone she handed to Jackson. "It's a replay of the Rangers' game from last night." She gently rubbed a spot of dirt off his cheek.

"Woohoo!" Jackson eagerly grabbed the phone and bent his head over it. Cormac could hear the crack of a bat hitting the ball after he pushed the play button.

Ellie finally glanced over at Cormac. "I'm sorry to be this much trouble."

"Oh!" He pretended to scowl at her. "Did you plan your son's asthma attack?"

She rolled her eyes at him. "Omigosh! You totally lied to my kid. You *are* a clown."

"Nah, I just happen to have five brothers. Hard not to turn into a smart aleck when you're surrounded by that many pranksters."

"Those are almost the same words my husband used when he was referring to his buddies in the SEALS." Her voice was sad. "They were like brothers, too."

For no particular reason, Cormac's heart sank at the mention of a husband. Then it dawned on him that she was speaking in the past tense. "Yeah, from what I've heard about the Navy SEALS, they're a tight group. Not surprised. It's a tough job. They gotta have each other's backs."

"They do. They risked everything to rescue him from behind enemy lines. They didn't make it in time, but they brought him back, anyway." The pain in her voice was so acute that it radiated all the way down to the toes in his boots.

"I'm sorry for your loss, ma'am."

"Thanks." She dabbed at the corners of her eyes and shot a furtive glance at her son. "The asthma attacks have gotten more frequent since the funeral. I'm a horrible mother for leaving his inhaler behind."

"Don't be so hard on yourself. You have a lot on your plate right now." He sought to steer the conversation to a more cheerful topic. "I hear you're helping your brother house shop."

"Not just him." She waved her hands at her face to finish drying her eyes. "Jackson and I are hunting for a house, as well."

Cormac's eyebrows shot upward. "You're moving to Chipper?" That was news to him — not unwelcome news, either.

"We're thinking about it." She smiled faintly. "As you've probably heard, my brother has accepted the superintendent position here, and he can be pretty persuasive when it comes to recruiting teachers. If I'm being honest, though, it wasn't a hard sell." She shot a concerned look at her son. "We could use a fresh start."

A half-dozen ways to help her find that fresh start popped into Cormac's mind — everything from inviting Ellie to sign Jackson up for the team he was coaching next season, to wheedling her into serving as their Team Mom.

Well, I'll be! He blinked at the realization that he was really looking forward to getting to know her better. Fox was going to have a heyday when he found out, especially after his warning about their mother's tricks. He could already hear his youngest brother's voice, asking him something stupid like: *So did the new chick finally rev that cranky old motor of yours?*

And Cormac would be lying through his teeth if he said no.

CHAPTER 10: PROOF OF LOVE

JADE

Later that evening

JADE'S MOTHER was worn out from the rodeo, but Jade had never seen her happier.

"Let me see that ring again." She reached for her daughter's hand. They were sharing a glass of iced tea in the living room with her father, Todd, and Ellie. Jackson was playing in the corner with one of the barn cats that someone had let in the house.

Feeling a tad guilty about brandishing her ring in front of Todd, Jade held out her hand so her mother could ooh and aah some more over her engagement ring.

"I've heard so many stories about Beldon's great-grandmother." Tandy Arletta gazed at the ring in wonder. "You're wearing the diamond of a real legend, hon. They say she herded cattle right alongside her husband and sons."

"I wish I could have met her." Jade shot an apologetic look at Todd and tried to change the subject. "So, did you enjoy your first Chipper rodeo, Superintendent Hoffman?"

"Very much." His expression was carefully bland. She could only imagine how disappointing it was for him to witness Beldon's marriage proposal after dropping so many hints to her about the possibility of dating her himself. "All's well that ends well, beautiful." He angled his head at the hand bearing her engagement ring. Her mother still had her hand imprisoned between both of her hands.

"We'll need to introduce you to some of our local single ladies soon." She watched him closely for a reaction.

There was none. "Don't mind if you do."

Yeah, he was hurt. He was being nice about it, but he was hurt. "We actually hosted a kissing booth at our last charity event. I'm already on the lookout for hunky volunteers for our next one."

Todd's gray eyes glinted with humor.

"No way!" Ellie chimed in. "A kissing booth?"

"An honest-to-heavens kissing booth. It was staffed solely by the Cassidy brothers last time." Jade felt a blush creep across her cheeks at the memory of the kiss she and Beldon had shared that day. "Which means we're down two whole kissers."

Todd snorted. "I'm not sure if I meet the requirement of hunky, but I might be persuaded if the cause is worthy enough."

He was interested. She could tell. "Are you kidding? All I would have to do is make a sign that reads, *Tall, Dark, and Handsome School Superintendent.* I guarantee you'll have a line at your booth that stretches from here to New Mexico."

"Now you're just messing with me." He wadded up the paper from his straw and tossed it at her.

She caught it. "There's one way to find out. That is, if you're not too chicken to pucker up," she taunted.

"Okay." Mischief flared in his gaze. "I'm in."

While she was inwardly congratulating herself on how easy it had been to recruit him for the next kissing booth, her phone rang. "Oops! Sorry. Forgot to turn down the ringer." Pulling her hand from her mother's grasp, she retrieved her cell phone from her purse and held it to her ear. "Hey! Jade speaking." Her heart raced, fully expecting to hear Beldon's voice in her ear.

It was Cormac, instead. "Uh, Jade?"

"What's going on?" She could tell something was wrong.

"It's about Beldon. There's been an accident."

A ripple of fear shot through her. "What do you mean, there's been an accident?" Her voice rose shrilly.

"We're not sure what happened yet. All I can tell you is, something spooked the herd. There was a stampede, and he's hurt real bad."

She felt the blood drain from her face. "I thought he had the day off for the rodeo," she choked. What in the world was he doing out in the field at this late hour?

"He got called in by one of the other range riders." Cormac's voice was sorrowful. "They've been having a lot of trouble lately with the coyotes."

"Where is he?" She half-rose to her feet, swaying slightly.

"They air-lifted him to Amarillo. Everyone else left for the hospital already. I can swing by to pick you up on my way, if you want to go."

"Yes! Yes, of course," she choked. He ended the call, and her cell phone fell from her nerveless fingers to the floor.

"Jade!" Todd flew across the room to take a knee in front of her. He returned her cell phone to her hand and curled her fingers around it. "What's wrong?"

"Beldon's been hurt. It's bad." Fear like she'd never known before clawed through her heart. "I just got him back! I can't lose him now." A sob wrenched itself from her. "I can't!"

———

Beldon's world was like an ocean of pain. As soon as he absorbed one wave of it, the next one crashed over him. They seemed to be growing in intensity. His legs felt like they were positively on fire. Though he couldn't open his eyes, he could hear the rumble of a helicopter overhead. The swirling wind and dust as it landed nearby stung his face and arms.

Hands lifted him and moved him to a stretcher, creating more screaming waves of pain. He might have actually screamed. He wasn't sure. Afterward, he drifted in and out of consciousness. Eventually, the pain stopped. It was replaced by bright lights and people in white uniforms. Lots and lots of people in white. At one point, he was staring right up at one of them before everything went black again.

It was hard to gauge how long he drifted. Sometimes he felt like he was rolling. Other times he was still. The fact that he could still feel the puncture of a needle in his arm was his only verification that he was still alive. Man, but he'd always hated IVs! The last time he'd been hooked up to one was when he'd suffered a bout of pneumonia as a teenager. Before that, he'd gotten overheated on the football field in junior high, and that had also resulted in an IV.

It took a massive amount of effort, but he finally found the strength to open his eyes. The breath eased out of his chest at the sight of both of his legs in casts. They looked like white logs suspended by silver cords from the ceiling. Fortunately, the oxygen mask covering his mouth kicked in and resupplied him with air.

"He's awake!" a woman's voice sobbed.

It was his mother, and she sounded close. Moments later, he realized why his left hand felt so warm. It was because she was gripping it.

"Mom?" His voice was muffled behind the mask.

"I'm here, baby."

He turned his head and found a very disheveled version of her watching him anxiously. Her makeup was smudged, and her hair was stringing around her pale cheeks.

In the minutes that followed, a doctor entered the room to speak to them, and the oxygen mask was lowered from his mouth so he could answer the man's questions.

"How do you feel, Beldon?"

"Groggy, sir." He couldn't feel his legs at all, which worried him. "Why can't I feel my legs?"

"Because the anesthesia is still wearing off. Believe me, the fact that you can't feel them right now is a good thing."

"Why?" Beldon demanded.

"You were hurt. Do you remember what happened?"

It made Beldon's head throb to think about it, but the memories slowly trickled back. "There was a pack of coyotes and a runaway horse." He blew out a breath. "One of the range riders got bucked off. I rode into the herd to extract him before he got trampled, and the next thing I knew…" He shook his head as he relived the horror of what happened next. "There was a stampede."

Turning to his mother, he inquired hastily, "Did Chuck make it out alive?" He remembered reaching the side of the unconscious range rider and leaping to the ground to scoop him up and toss him over his horse like a sack of potatoes. Everything after that was a blur.

"Yes, baby. Thanks to you." His mother gripped his hand tighter. "He's pretty banged up, but he's going to pull through. We've had people praying around the clock for both of you."

"Around the clock?" He frowned at her. "How long was I out?"

"Two of the longest days of my life." Her voice shook. "But you're awake, and you're going to be okay now. Right, doctor?"

The man nodded gravely. "You're through the riskiest part, that's for sure, but not the hardest part."

"What do you mean?" his mother asked nervously.

The doctor moved to stand beside Beldon's bed, so he could look him directly in the eye. "You almost lost your left leg, son. If you want any hope of walking again, you've got a battle ahead. Some of it will take place in the physical therapy unit — a few months' worth, actually. Most of it will take place right here." He leaned over to lightly tap Beldon's temple.

I'm an invalid. Beldon's father stepped into the room, looking every ounce as haggard as his mother. *I'm a freaking invalid!* Anger churned in his gut at the unfairness of it all. *I was supposed to marry Jade soon, and now I might never walk again.*

Fear chased the anger. He knew it was probably just the anesthesia messing with his head, but he couldn't help wondering if Jade would have it in her to remain by his side. From the sound of things, he might actually end up in a wheelchair.

After the doctor left the room, his brothers filed in next, ashen faced and exhausted. Asher approached the bed first. He cupped the back of Beldon's head and lightly tapped their foreheads together. "Welcome back. You gave us a pretty big scare." His voice was rough with emotion.

His brothers took turns bumping his fist and squeezing his shoulders.

Beldon appreciated their love and concern, but the face that was missing from the room bothered him the most.

"Where's Jade?" he grated out.

Silence fell over his family as they glanced at each other.

"Where is she?" he demanded in a louder voice.

"With her mother," Ridge Cassidy informed him quietly. "Tandy took a turn for the worse and had to be admitted to the hospital last night."

Beldon swung his head from side-to-side in agitation. "I should be with her," he growled. Instead, he was tied down with too many cords and wires to count. He'd never before felt so helpless.

"She's here," his mother assured gently. "Only a few floors down from us. I'll let her know you're awake. I just wanted to make sure you were ready for...company first."

The hesitation in her voice was puzzling. "She's not company, Mom. She's the woman I'm going to marry."

"Of course she is, baby. That's what I meant." Though her words were reassuring, the anxious light didn't leave her eyes.

Beldon glanced around the room to discover all

five of his brothers were having a hard time meeting his gaze. He stared at them in disappointment. "You don't think she'll come visit me, do you?"

Asher shrugged. "I don't think hospitals are her thing, bro. She didn't spend much time here when I was the one lying where you are." They'd been dating at the time, too.

Beldon couldn't believe the way his family was acting. It was Jade they were talking about. She wouldn't abandon him at a time like this. She loved him too much, and she was better than that. Back when Asher was in the hospital was an entirely different situation, because she'd been planning on breaking up with him before he got injured. Even so, the expressions on the faces of his family members right now were beginning to worry him. Had something happened between them and Jade in the past two days that they weren't telling him?

"Just tell her I'm awake, will you?" He hated how hoarse he sounded. They were wrong about her, and he was going to prove it.

"Already done." Claire Cassidy waved her cell phone in the air. "Uh, how about the rest of us figure out what we're going to do for lunch?" She shot a warning look at his brothers that emptied out the room in record time. Her phone buzzed with a message. She glanced at the screen, brightening considerably. "Jade is on her way up to see you. Your dad and I will be right around the corner if you need anything."

"Hold up!" he croaked.

"What is it, baby?" She paused in her promenade to the door.

"A little help, please?" He flailed for the glass of water on his nightstand. "I need to brush my teeth and untangle my hair before she gets here."

Man, but it was awkward performing simple tasks like that while lying horizontal! However, his parents made short work of it.

When the door finally closed behind them, he was relieved. The doubt they were exhibiting about Jade was beginning to make him doubt, too. He hated himself for feeling that way, but maybe they were right. Maybe he was being naive. Maybe he'd foolishly and blindly loved Jade for so many years that he couldn't see the truth.

A soft knock sounded on the other side of the door. Before he could answer, it opened a crack. "It's me. Jade." She pushed the door open wider.

"Oh, Beldon!" She stumbled across the threshold, looking so ravaged that his heart shook beneath his ribs.

"Jade!" he rasped, reaching for her.

She flew in his direction in a rumpled green silk shirt that was coming untucked from her jeans. "When I heard you were awake, I…" She was unable to finish the sentence. Reaching his bed, she sank down beside him and slid her arms around his middle. "I can't lose you, Beldon!" She collapsed against his chest, pressing her cheek against his hospital gown, directly over his heart.

Relief flooded him so strongly that it made him

lightheaded for a few seconds. She still loved him. That was all that mattered. Everything else they would figure out. Eventually.

"You're not going to lose me, darlin'." He buried his hands in her hair, gently massaging her scalp as she dissolved into silent sobs.

It was several minutes before she could raise her head. Fixing her tear-drenched gaze on his, she murmured, "I'm sorry for falling apart like this. You're the one who's hurt."

It was obvious to him that he wasn't the only one who was hurting, though. He could only imagine what she'd been through in the past two days with both her fiancé and mother landing in the hospital.

He cupped her face in his hands. "I'm fine. How's Tandy?"

More tears dripped from her eyes, telling him that her mother's condition wasn't good. "You're not fine," she choked, "and neither is she."

"We're going to get through this, darlin'." He couldn't promise her that her mother would get better on this side of Glory, but he sure as heck intended to climb out of this bed soon.

"I've been so afraid, Beldon." Jade's words came out in a rush. "For you. For us. For my family and yours." With a strangled sob, she leaned closer to press her trembling lips to his. "I love you so much!"

He savored the feel of her warm mouth and the salty taste of her tears. As her lips moved against his, he felt a surge of strength return to his limbs and a spiral of hope shoot through his chest. As long as he had her in his life, he had a reason to keep fighting.

"I love you, too." He spoke against her lips, silently thanking the Lord that he was still alive. Even if he had to support Jade from a blasted wheelchair in the coming days, he intended to be there for her and her family.

"I need you so much, Beldon." Her lips traveled over his face, brushing against his eyelids, the tip of his nose, and down his jawline. "Don't ever scare me like that again. My heart can't take it."

"Yes, ma'am." He palmed the back of her neck and brought her mouth back to his.

EPILOGUE

IN THE DAYS and weeks following Beldon's accident, the citizens of Chipper didn't go easy on Jade. Rumors flew fast and thick that she would break up with "that poor, sweet cowboy" now that he was damaged, the same way she'd done with his oldest brother.

Jade tried to ignore them, but it was hard. As she was preparing to drive Beldon to his physical therapy appointment one afternoon, she'd had more than she could take of their sarcasm. Flinging open her closet door, she rummaged through her clothing for something guaranteed to get their tongues wagging in a different direction. Her gaze landed on a short, black leather skirt. *Oh, yeah!* She quickly paired it with a glossy red silk blouse and matching stilettos.

It was time to show the world that she and Beldon were still very much in love, and she couldn't think of a better way of doing that than by dressing as if they were going on a date.

When she drove up to Beldon's two-story log cabin and stepped from the car, he was already rolling his wheelchair out of his garage. He stopped short and simply stared at her.

She leaned back against her Jaguar, knowing she looked her best. "See something you like, cowboy?"

"Hoh, yeah!" Blue eyes glinting with pleasure, he rolled closer. "What's the occasion?"

"Today you're going to stand again."

He raised his dark eyebrows at her. "With the help of bars, maybe."

She shrugged. "We gotta start somewhere." He did most of the work as she helped him slide his broad frame into the passenger seat. Somehow, she ended up on his lap.

"Beldon," she gasped. "I don't want to re-injure anything."

"You won't," he assured huskily, gathering her close. "The bones are almost completely healed. I just have to train the muscles and ligaments how to walk again."

"Okay. I just wanted to be sure," she murmured as his mouth slowly descended toward hers.

"If you didn't want to end up exactly where you are, you shouldn't have dressed the way you did." He gently plundered her lips, deepening the kiss and drinking her in like he was dying of thirst.

"Savage," she teased when he came up for air.

"You started it by attacking me in your own car." He tangled one large hand in her hair.

"Hey, now! You pulled me into your lap, cowboy, not the other way around."

"You have no proof." He swooped in for another kiss that curled her toes in her sandals.

"I'm so glad you're better," she sighed against his lips.

"What can I say? You inspire me." He tipped his forehead against hers, breathing her in.

"I can't take credit. It's nothing short of a miracle, and I'm more thankful than words can express."

"Love is a miracle, Jade." He ran his thumb along the underside of her chin. "And, yes, you inspire me. I can't tell you how much it means to me the way you've stuck by my side, not knowing for sure if I'll ever walk again."

"You will," she assured with conviction.

"But if I don't?" He sobered.

"Then you'll be taking me on a lot of carriage rides, cowboy." She punctuated the directive with a kiss. "And a few sleigh rides." She kissed him again.

"I will," he promised, trailing the back of his hand down her cheek. "But just so you know, I intend to carry my wife to those carriages and sleigh rides, because I fully intend to walk again. The doc says I have a 95% chance at this point of getting the full range of motion back in my legs."

She drew back, since it was the first time she was hearing that number. "When did he say that?"

"Yesterday." He gazed deeply into her eyes.

"And you're just now telling me this?" she cried, wondering why he would keep something so wonderful from her.

"I wanted to know how you felt about marrying a guy who might not walk again."

"Not a guy," she fumed. "You! I'm marrying you, Beldon, and no one else. Yes, I hope and pray that you'll be able to walk again, but it won't change the way that I feel about you if it doesn't happen."

"Good. Because I wasn't planning on letting you go, no matter what."

———————

The physical therapist chuckled as Jade walked beside Beldon while he wheeled himself into the gym. He shot an admiring look at her. "I hear you're recovering in leaps and bounds, Mr. Cassidy." He handed Beldon his first workout regimen. "That said, don't expect me to go easy on you today."

At one point, the physical therapist had Beldon propped on a pair of parallel bars, walking slowing forward while balancing most of his weight on his arms.

Beldon knew he was being cocky, but he made sure he did plenty of flexing for Jade's benefit.

She clapped her hands in delight when he reached the end of the bars. "Okay. I'm just going to say it. That was hot!" She stepped forward to plant a kiss on his lips.

Wishing his arms were around her, he did the

next best thing and deepened the kiss. The rest of the patients in the room clapped and cheered, egging him on.

His physical therapist was grinning from ear to ear by the time they finished the full workout session. "You inspired a lot of patients here today, Mr. Cassidy and Miss Arletta. I am beginning to understand the reasons behind your rapid recovery, Mr. Cassidy."

On their drive home, Beldon reached across the console to lace his fingers through hers. "I suspect you started a few new rumors around town today."

"That was the idea." Her lips twisted in a pout. "I've had enough of the smack talk about our relationship. What we have is beautiful and real. I'm so thankful to have you in my life that it kills me when people try to talk it down. They couldn't be more wrong about us. If you'd felt up to it, I seriously would've married you the day you woke up in the hospital."

He brought her fingers to his lips, marveling at her vehemence. "Let's do it, Jade. Let's get married."

She hit the brakes a little harder than she meant to at the next stop sign. "Now?"

"Why not?" He shrugged. "We applied for our marriage license weeks ago."

"Because your mother would pull one of her rifles out of the gun cabinet and plug holes in both of us," she breathed.

He knew she was thinking of stuff like flowers,

cakes, and dresses. "Your mother would talk her out of it," he retorted gently.

Hating to bring up a reminder that Tandy wasn't getting any better, he watched Jade catch her lower lip between her teeth. "You're right," she whispered. "I didn't want to rush things before you were ready, but that's been one of my biggest fears since the accident. That my mom wouldn't be here when we finally..." Her voice faded. "I don't have anything planned, though. I don't even have a dress."

He burst out laughing. "You have a million dresses. I'm going to have to put an addition on the house to hold all of them."

She shot him a pouty look. "I meant a wedding dress."

He arched an eyebrow at her. "Aren't you and Bella about the same size?"

She caught her breath, eyes widening in speculation. "That might actually work. You're an absolute genius, Beldon Cassidy!"

"Not even close."

He could sense her mind racing as her organizational skills kicked in. "I'll make a few calls about the cake and flowers."

He squeezed her fingers, hardly believing she was seriously considering his idea to tie the knot this soon. "I'll see what the minister's schedule looks like."

———

Two days later, Luis Arletta brought his wife home from the hospital beneath the ministration of a hospice care nurse. Their closest friends were already gathered on the front lawn beneath a white canopy.

Under Jade's direction, the florist had draped red and white rose blooms and vines around the porch railing and columns. A matching rose trellis anchored the sidewalk below the steps. The minister stood beneath it with his Bible open in his hands.

Bella was wearing the maid of honor dress that Jade had worn to her wedding only weeks earlier. From her perch on a stool beside the rose trellis, she strummed her guitar through the opening chords of the bridal march.

Beldon, who'd been sitting in his wheelchair in front of the rose trellis, nodded at his brothers. Asher and Cormac hurried forward, lugging a pair of sawhorses. They positioned them in front of the minister, and Beldon used them to hoist himself to his feet. Asher rolled the wheelchair a few feet away, but he didn't go far. He remained poised to rush it back at a moment's notice.

Bracing most of his weight on his arms, Beldon gazed in wonder at his bride as she glided toward him on her father's arm. Though he'd seen it one other time, the dress she was wearing looked entirely different with her in it. It hugged her slender curves while the hem of her full skirt dragged the grass with each sashaying step that brought her closer to him.

When they reached the rose trellis, Luis reached out to clasp Beldon's shoulder. "I couldn't have picked a better man to marry my daughter." His dark eyes glistened. "Take care of her for me, son."

"I will, sir." He and Jade smiled at each other as she waited for him to pivot around on the sawhorses to face the minister. One of the sawhorses rocked a little in the process, making their family and guests gasp in alarm.

Jade and the minister both lunged for it and held it steady until he was facing forward. Then her hand curled gently around his arm.

"Make it quick!" she hissed to the minister.

Beldon's grin widened, knowing she was worried about how long he could stand between the sawhorses. She was truly amazing. The fact that she was about to become his wife was mind-boggling.

At her insistence, the minister kept the ceremony blessedly short. The moment they finished their vows, Asher shoved the wheelchair back beneath him and carted off the sawhorses.

There was an awkward pause before the minister announced, "I now pronounce you husband and wife." He turned to Jade. "You may kiss your groom."

She promptly took a seat in Beldon's lap, fanning her full lacy skirt around them. Whether she meant to or not, it hid the wheels of his chair from view.

The kiss she gave him left no doubt in his mind — and hopefully the minds of everyone present — that she was very much in love with her range rider. The way he kissed her back must have been equally convincing to those who witnessed it.

"They're so much in love," one woman sighed.

"Yes, we are." He nuzzled Jade's lips. "Forever and always."

"Forever and always," she echoed, giving him one more soft peck. Then she leaned back in his arms to give him an impish smile. "Does this mean I can finally decorate your pitifully bare bachelor's pad?"

"It's a married man's pad now, but yes." He couldn't wait to see what she had in mind, knowing she was more than capable of turning his house into a real home. "Have at it, Mrs. Cassidy. It's all yours, and so am I."

The dreamy smile she sent him was a promise that she was every bit as much his and always would be.

———

Like this book? Leave a review now!

Ready to find out how Cormac plans to convince single mom Ellie to date again? Or (to be more specific) to date him!
Check out
Mr. Right But She Doesn't Know It.

Much love,
Jo

NOTE FROM JO

Don't worry! There's a lot more going on at Cassidy Farm, and you don't have to wait until the next book to read it.

Because...*drum roll*...I have some Bonus Content for

you. Find out what *else* happened between Cormac and Ellie on the drive back to the ranch that really got his motor revving (as he likes to call it) by signing up for my mailing list. There will be a special bonus content for each COWBOY CONFESSIONS book, just for my subscribers. Also, you'll hear about my next new book as soon as it's out *(plus you get a free book)*. Woohoo!

As always, thank you for reading and loving my books!

JOIN CUPPA JO READERS!

If you're on Facebook, please join my group, Cuppa Jo Readers. Don't miss out on the giveaways + all the sweet and swoony cowboys!

https://www.facebook.com/groups/
CuppaJoReaders

GET A FREE BOOK!

Join my mailing list to be the first to know about new releases, free books, special discount prices, and other giveaways.

https://BookHip.com/JNNHTK

SNEAK PREVIEW: MR. RIGHT BUT SHE DOESN'T KNOW IT

" Cowboy Confessions "

WHEN YOU FALL *head over heels for a hot single mom who insists she'll never date again — but you're determined to change her mind!*

Cormac makes it clear to his brothers that he's not interested in being the next one to get hitched. He's met every cowgirl in their small Texas town, and he's very sure none of them are *the one*. Until Ellie Roberts shows up at their charity rodeo with her six-year-old in the middle of an asthma attack.

Farmer and crop duster pilot by day and Little League coach by night, Cormac fortunately knows how to perform first aid on young baseball players. Call it a perk that the kid's mother is sweet and friendly with such sad, beautiful eyes that he finds himself doing everything he can to make her smile again. And convince her to serve as his next Team Mom. And join him on a dinner date that ends with a goodnight kiss or two or ten.

Okay, so maybe the dinner date and kisses are only wishful thinking on his part, but farmers happen to know a thing or two about how to make things grow. He's hoping if he sows the seeds of friendship, showers her with all the time and attention he can carve out of his busy schedule, then maybe he can get her feelings for him to blossom into something more.

A sweet and inspirational, small-town romance with a few Texas-sized detours into comedy!

———

Mr. Right But She Doesn't Know It
Available in eBook, paperback, and Kindle Unlimited!

Mr. Not Right for Her
Mr. Maybe Right for Her
Mr. Right But She Doesn't Know It
Mr. Right Again for Her
Mr. Yeah, Right. As If...

Much love,
Jo

SNEAK PREVIEW: ACCIDENTAL HERO

MATT ROMERO WAS SINGLE AGAIN, and this time he planned to stay that way.

Feeling like the world's biggest fool, he gripped the steering wheel of his white Ford F-150, cruising up the sunny interstate toward Amarillo. He had an interview in the morning, so he was arriving a day early to get the lay of the land. That, and he was anxious to put as many miles as possible between him and his ex.

It was one thing to have allowed himself to become blinded by love. It was another thing entirely to have fallen for the stupidest line in a cheater's handbook.

Cat sitting. I actually allowed her to talk me into cat sitting! Plus, he'd collected his fiancée's mail and carried her latest batch of Amazon deliveries into her condo.

It wasn't that he minded helping out the woman he planned to spend the rest of his life with. What he minded was that she wasn't in New York City on business like she'd claimed. *Nope.* As it turned out, she was nowhere near the Big Apple. It had simply been her cover story for cheating on him, the first lie in a long series of lies.

To make matters worse, she'd recently talked Matt into leaving the Army for her, a decision he'd probably regret for the rest of his life now that she'd broken their engagement and moved on with someone else.

Leaving me single, jobless, and —

The scream of sirens jolted Matt back to the present. A glance in his rearview mirror confirmed his suspicions. He was getting pulled over. *For what?* A scowl down at his speedometer revealed he was cruising at no less than 95 mph. *Whoa!* It was a good twenty miles over the posted speed limit. *Okay, this is bad.* He'd be lucky if he didn't lose his license over this — his fault entirely for driving distracted without his cruise control on. *My day just keeps getting better.*

Slowing and pulling his truck over to the shoulder, he coasted to a stop and waited. And waited. And waited some more. A peek in his side mirror showed the cop was still sitting in his car and talking on his phone.

Oh, come on! Just give me my ticket already.

To stop the pounding between his temples, Matt reached for the red cooler he'd propped on the passenger seat and pulled out a can of soda. He popped the tab and tipped it up to chug down a shot of caffeine. He hadn't slept much the last couple of nights.

Before he could take a second sip, movement in the rearview mirror caught his attention. He watched as the police officer finally opened his door, unfolded his large frame from the front seat of his black SUV, and stood. However, he continued talking on his phone instead of walking Matt's way.

Are you kidding me? Matt swallowed a dry chuckle and took another swig of his soda. It was a good thing he'd hit the road the day before his interview at the Pantex nuclear plant. At the rate his day was going, it might take the rest of the afternoon to collect his speeding ticket.

He'd reached the outskirts of Amarillo, only about twenty to thirty miles from his final destination. The exit sign for Hereford was up ahead. Or the Beef Capital of the World, as the small farm town was often called.

He reached across the dashboard to open his glove compartment and fish out his registration card and proof of insurance. His gut told him there wasn't going to be any talking his way out of this one. As a general rule, men in blue didn't sympathize with folks going twenty miles or more over the speed limit.

Digging for his wallet, he pulled out his driver's license. Out of sheer habit, he reached inside the slot where he normally kept his military ID and found it empty. *Right.* He no longer possessed one, which left him with an oddly empty feeling.

He took another gulp of soda and watched as the officer pocketed his cell phone. *Finally! Guess that means it's time to get this party started.* Matt chunked his soda can into the nearest cup holder and stuck his driver's license, truck registration, and insurance card between two fingers. Hitting an automatic button on the door, he lowered his window a few inches and waited.

The guy strode up to Matt's truck window with a bit of a swagger. His tan Stetson was pulled low over his eyes. "License and registration, soldier."

Guess you noticed the Ranger tab on my license plate. Matt wordlessly poked the requested items through the window opening.

"Any reason you're in such a hurry this morning?" the officer mused curiously as he scanned Matt's identification. He was so tall, he had to stoop to peer through the window. Like Matt, he had a dark tan, brown hair, and a goatee. The two of them could've passed as cousins or something.

"Nothing worth hearing, officer." *My problem. Not yours. Don't want to talk about it.* Matt squinted through the glaring sun to read the guy's name on his tag. *McCarty.*

"That's too bad, because I always have plenty of time to chat when I'm writing up such a hefty ticket." Officer McCarty's tone was mildly sympathetic, though it was impossible to read his expression behind his sunglasses. "I clocked you going twenty-two miles over the posted limit, Mr. Romero."

Twenty-two miles? Yeah, that's not good. Not good at

all. Matt's jaw tightened, and he could feel the veins in his temples throbbing. It looked like he was going to have to share his story, after all. Maybe, just maybe, the trooper would feel so sorry for him that he'd give him a warning instead of a ticket. It was worth a try, anyway. *If nothing else, it'll give you something to laugh about during your next coffee break.*

"Today was supposed to be my wedding day." He spoke through stiff lips, finding a strange sort of relief in confessing that sorry fact to a perfect stranger. Fortunately, they'd never have to see each other again.

"I'm sorry for your loss." Officer McCarty glanced up from Matt's license to give him what felt like a piercing once over. He was probably trying to gauge if he was telling the truth or not.

"Oh, she's still alive," Matt muttered. "Found somebody else, that's all." He gripped the steering wheel and drummed his thumbs against it. *I'm just the poor fool she cheated on.*

He was so done with dating. At the moment, he couldn't imagine ever again putting his heart on the chopping block of love. *Better to be lonely than to let another person destroy you like that.* She'd taken everything from him that mattered — his pride, his dignity, even his career.

"Ouch," Officer McCarty sighed. "Well, here comes the tough part about my job. Despite your reasons for speeding, you were putting lives at risk. Your own included."

"Can't disagree with that." Matt stared straight

ahead, past the small spidery nick in his windshield. He'd gotten hit by a rock earlier while passing a semi tractor trailer. It really hadn't been his day. Or his week. Or his year, for that matter. It didn't mean he was going to grovel, though. He'd tried to appeal to the guy's sympathy and failed. The sooner he gave him his ticket, the sooner they could both be on their way.

A massive dump truck on the oncoming side of the highway abruptly swerved into the narrow, grassy median. It was a few hundred yards away, but the front left tire dipped down, *way* down, making the truck pitch heavily to one side.

"Whoa!" Matt shouted, pointing to get Officer McCarty's attention. "That guy looks like he's in trouble!"

Two vehicles on Matt's side of the road passed him in quick succession — a rusty blue van pulling a fifth wheel and a shiny red Dodge Ram.

When Officer McCarty didn't respond, Matt laid on his horn to warn the two drivers, just as the dump truck started to roll. It was like watching a horror movie in slow motion, knowing something bad was about to happen while being helpless to stop it.

The dump truck slammed onto its side and skidded noisily across Matt's lane. The blue van whipped to the right shoulder in a vain attempt to avoid the collision. Matt winced as the van's bumper caught the hood of the skidding dump truck nearly head on, then jack-knifed into the air.

The driver of the red truck was only a few car

lengths behind, jamming so hard on its brakes that it left two dark smoking lines of rubber on the pavement. Seconds later, it careened into the median and flipped on its side. It wasn't immediately clear if the red pickup had collided with any part of the dump truck. However, an ominous swirl of smoke seeped from beneath its hood.

For a split second, Matt and Officer McCarty stared in shock at each other. Then the officer shoved Matt's license and registration back through the opening in the window. "Looks like I've got more important things to do than give you a ticket." He sprinted toward his SUV, leaped inside, and gunned it toward the scene of the accident with his lights flashing and sirens blaring. He only drove a short distance before stopping his vehicle and canting it across both lanes to form a makeshift blockade.

Though Matt was no longer in the military, his defend-and-protect instincts kicked in. There was no telling how long it would take the emergency vehicles to arrive, and he didn't like the way the red pickup was smoking. The driver hadn't climbed out of the cab yet, either, which wasn't a good sign.

Officer McCarty reached the blue van first, probably because it was the closest, and assisted a dazed man from one of the back passenger seats. He led him to the side of the road, helped him get seated on a small incline, then jogged back to help the driver exit the van. Unfortunately, the officer was only one man, and this was much bigger than a one-man job.

Following his gut instincts, Matt disengaged his

emergency brake and gunned his way up the shoulder, pausing beside the officer's vehicle. Turning off his motor, he leaped from his truck and jogged across the highway to the red pickup. The motor was still running, and the smoke was rising more thickly now.

Whoever was behind the wheel needed to get out immediately before the thing caught fire or exploded. Matt took a flying leap to hop on top of the cab and crawl to the driver's door. It was locked.

Pounding on the window, he shouted at the driver, "You okay in there?"

There was no answer and no movement. Peering closer, he could make out the unmoving figure of a woman. Blonde, pale, and curled to one side. The only thing holding her in place was the strap of a seatbelt around her waist. A trickle of red ran across one cheek.

Matt's survival training kicked in. Crouching over the side of the truck, he quickly assessed the undamaged windshield and decided it wasn't the best entry point. *Too bad.* Because his only other option was to shower the driver with glass. *Sorry, lady!* Swinging a leg, he jabbed the heel of his boot into the section of window nearest the lock. By some miracle, he managed to pop a fist-sized hole instead of shattering the entire pane.

Reaching inside, he unlocked the door and pulled it open. The next part was a little trickier, since he had to reach down, *way* down, to unbuckle the woman and catch her weight before she fell. It would've been easier if she were conscious and able to follow his instructions.

Guess I'll have to do it without any help. An ominous hiss of steam and smoke from beneath the hood stiffened his resolve and made him move faster.

"Come on, lady," he muttered, releasing her seatbelt and catching her slender frame before she fell. With a grunt of exertion, he hefted her free of the mangled cab. Then he half-slid, half hopped back to the ground with her in his arms. As soon as his boots hit the pavement, he took off at a jog.

She was lighter than he'd been expecting. Her upper arm, that his left hand was cupped around, felt desperately thin despite her baggy pink and plaid shirt. One long, strawberry blonde braid dangled over her shoulder, and a sprinkle of freckles stood out in stark relief against her pale cheeks.

She didn't so much as twitch as he ran with her, telling him that she was still out cold. He hoped it didn't mean she'd hit her head too hard on impact. Visions of traumatic brain injuries and their long list of complications swarmed through his mind, along with the possibility that he might've just finished moving a woman with a broken neck or back. *Please don't let that be the case, Lord.*

He carried her to the far right shoulder and up a grassy knoll where Officer McCarty was depositing the other injured victims. A dry wind gusted, sending a layer of fine dust in their direction. One prickly, rolling tumbleweed followed. On the other side of the knoll was a rocky canyon wall that went straight up, underscoring the fact that there really hadn't been any way for the hapless van and pickup drivers to avoid the collision. They'd literally been trapped between the canyon and oncoming traffic.

An explosion ricocheted through the air, shaking the ground beneath Matt's feet. On pure instinct, he dove for the grass, using his body to shield the woman in his arms. He used one hand to cradle her head against his chest and his other hand to break their fall as best he could.

A few of the other injured drivers and passengers cried out in fear as smoke billowed around them and blanketed the scene. For the next few minutes, it was difficult to see much, though the wave of ensuing heat had a suffocating feel to it. The woman beneath Matt remained motionless, though he thought he heard her mumble something at one point. He continued to crouch over her, keeping her head cradled beneath his hand. He rubbed his thumb beneath her nose and determined she was still breathing. However, she remained unconscious. He debated what to do next.

A fire engine howled in the distance, making his shoulders slump in relief. Help had finally arrived. More sirens blared, and the area was soon crawling with fire engines, ambulances, and paramedics with stretchers. One walked determinedly in his direction.

"Hi! My name is Star, and I'm here to help you. What's your name, sir?" the EMT worker inquired in a calm, even tone. Her chin-length dark hair was blowing nearly sideways in the wind. She shook her head to knock it away, revealing a pair of snapping dark eyes swimming with concern.

"I'm Sergeant Matt Romero," he informed her out of sheer habit. *Well, maybe no longer the sergeant part.* "Don't worry about me. I'm fine. This woman is not. I don't know her name. She was unconscious when I pulled her out of her truck."

As the curvy EMT stepped closer, Matt could read her name tag. *Corrigan.* "Like I said, I'm here to do everything I can to help." Her forehead wrinkled in alarm as she caught sight of the injured woman's face. "Omigosh! Bree?" Tossing her red medical bag on the ground, she slid to her knees beside the two of them. "Oh, Bree, honey!" she sighed, reaching for her pulse.

"I-I..." The woman stirred. Her lashes fluttered a few times against her cheeks. Then they snapped open, revealing two pools of the deepest blue Matt had ever seen. Though glazed with pain, her gaze latched anxiously onto him. "Don't leave me," she pleaded with a hitch in her voice.

There was something oddly personal about the request. Though he was sure they'd never met before, she spoke as if she recognized him. Her confusion tugged at every one of his heartstrings, making him long to grant her request.

"I won't," he promised huskily, hardly knowing what he was saying. In that moment, he probably would have said anything to make the desperate look in her eyes go away.

"I'm not liking her heart rate." Star produced a

penlight and flipped it on. Shining it in one of her friend's eyes, then the other, she cried urgently, "Bree? It's me, Star. Can you tell me what happened, hon?"

A shiver worked its way through Bree's too-thin frame. "Don't leave me," she whispered again to Matt, before her eyelids fluttered closed. Another shiver worked its way through her, despite the fact that she was no longer conscious.

"She's going into shock." Star glanced worriedly over her shoulder. "Need a stretcher over here," she called sharply. One was swiftly rolled their way.

Matt helped the EMT lift and deposit their precious burden on it.

"Can you make it to the hospital?" Star asked as he helped push the stretcher toward the nearest ambulance. "Bree seemed pretty insistent about you sticking around."

Matt's eyebrows shot upward in surprise. He hadn't been expecting yet another person he'd never met before to ask him to stick around. "Uh, sure." In her delirium, the injured woman had probably mistaken him for someone else. However, he didn't mind helping out. *Who knows?* Maybe he could give the attending physician some information about her rescue that might prove useful in her treatment.

Or maybe he was just drawn to the fragile-looking Bree for reasons he couldn't explain. Whatever the case, Matt suddenly wasn't feeling in a terrible hurry to hit the road again. Fortunately, he had plenty of extra time built into his schedule before his interview tomorrow. The only real task he had left for the day was finding a hotel room once he reached Amarillo.

"I just need to let Officer McCarty know I'm leaving the scene of the accident." Matt shook his head sheepishly. "I kinda hate to admit this, but he had me pulled over for speeding before everything went down here." He waved a hand at the carnage around them. It was a dismal scene, punctuated by twisted metal and scorched pavement. All three mangled vehicles looked like they were totaled.

Star snickered, then seemed to catch herself. "Sorry. That was inappropriate laughter. Very inappropriate laughter."

He shrugged, not the least bit offended. A lot of people laughed when they were nervous or upset, which Star clearly had been since the moment she'd discovered the unconscious woman was a friend. "It was pretty stupid of me to be driving these long, empty stretches of highway without my cruise control on." Especially with the way he'd been brooding non-stop for the past seventy-two hours.

Star shot him a sympathetic look. "Believe me, I'm not judging. Far from it." She reached out to pat Officer McCarty's arm as they passed by him with the stretcher. "The only reason a bunch of us in Hereford don't have a lot more points on our licenses is because we grew up with this sweet guy."

"Oh, no! Is that Bree?" Officer McCarty groaned. He pulled his sunglasses down to take a closer look over the top of his lenses. His stoic expression was gone. In its place was one etched with worry. The personal kind. Like Star, he knew the victim.

"Yeah." Star's pink glossy lips twisted. "She and her brother can't catch a break, can they?"

Since two more paramedics converged on them to help lift Bree's stretcher into the ambulance, Matt paused to face the trooper who'd pulled him over.

"Any issues with me following them to the hospital, officer? Star asked me if I would." Unfortunately, it would give the guy more time and opportunity to ticket Matt, but that couldn't be helped.

"Emmitt," Officer McCarty corrected. "The name is Emmitt, alright? I think you more than worked off your ticket back there."

Sucking in a breath of relief, Matt held out a hand. "Thanks, man. I really appreciate it." It was a huge concession. The guy could've taken his license if he'd wanted to.

They soberly shook hands, eyeing each other.

"You need me to come by the PD to file a witness report or anything before I boogie out of town this evening?" Matt pressed.

"Nah. Just give me a call, and we'll take care of it over the phone." Emmitt produced a business card and handed it over. "Not sure if we'll need your story, since I saw it go down, but we should probably still cross every T."

"Roger that." Matt stuffed the card in the back pocket of his jeans.

"Where are you headed, anyway?"

"Amarillo. Got an interview at Pantex tomorrow."

"Nice! It's a solid company." Emmitt nodded. "I've got several friends who work there."

Star leaned out from the back of the ambulance. "You coming or what?" she called impatiently to Matt.

He nodded vigorously. "I'll follow you," he called back and jogged back to his truck. Since the ambulance was on the opposite side of the highway, he turned on his blinker and put his oversized tires to good use while traversing the median. He had to spin his wheels a bit in the center of the median to get his tires to grab the sandy incline leading to the other side. He was grateful all over again that he'd splurged on a few upgrades for his truck to make it fit for off-roading.

He followed the ambulance north and found himself driving the final twenty minutes or so to Amarillo, probably because it boasted a much bigger hospital than any of the smaller surrounding towns — more than one, actually. Due to another vehicle leaving the parking lot as he was entering it, Matt was able to grab a decently close parking spot. He jogged into the waiting room, dropped Star Corrigan's name a few times, and tried to make it sound like he was a close friend of the patient.

Looking doubtful, the receptionist made him wait while she paged Star, who appeared a short time later to escort him into the emergency room. "Bree's in Bay 6," she informed him in a strained voice, reaching for his arm and practically dragging him behind the curtain.

If anything, Bree looked even thinner and more fragile than she had outside on the highway. A nurse was stooped over her, inserting an I.V. into her arm.

"She still hasn't woken up." Star's voice was soft, barely above a whisper. "They're pretty sure she has a concussion. Sounds like they're gonna run a full battery of tests to figure out what's going on."

Matt nodded, not knowing what to say.

The lovely EMT's pager went off. She snatched it up and scowled at it. "I just got another call. It's a busy day out there for motorists." She texted a message on her cell phone, then cast him a sideways glance. "Any chance you'll be able to stick around until Bree's brother gets here?"

That's when it hit Matt that this had been the EMT's real goal all along — to ensure that her friend wasn't left alone. She'd known she could get called away to the next job at any second.

"Not a problem." He offered what he hoped was a reassuring smile. Amarillo was where he'd been heading, so he'd already reached his final destination. "I wasn't planning on going far, anyway. Got an interview at Pantex in the morning."

"No kidding! Well, good luck with that," she returned with a curious, searching look. "A lot of my friends moved up this way for jobs after high school."

Officer Emmitt McCarty had said something similar. "Hey, ah…" Matt hated detaining the EMT any longer than necessary, but it might not hurt to know a few more details about the unconscious woman, since he was about to be alone with her. "Mind telling me Bree's last name?"

"Anderson. Her brother is Brody. Brody Anderson. They run a ranch about halfway between here and Hereford, so it'll take him a good twenty to thirty minutes to get here."

"It's alright. I can stay. It was nice meeting you, by the way." His gaze landed on Bree's left hand, which was resting limply atop the white blankets on her bed. She wasn't wearing a wedding ring. *Not that it matters. I'm a complete idiot for looking.* He forced his gaze back to the EMT. "Sorry about the circumstances, of course."

"Me, too." She shot another worried look at her friend and dropped her voice conspiratorially. "Hey, you're really not supposed to be back here since you're not family, but I sorta begged and they sorta agreed to overlook the rules until Brody gets here." She eyed him worriedly.

"Don't worry." He could tell she hated the necessity of leaving. "I'll stick around until her brother gets here, even if I get booted out to the waiting room with the regular Joes."

"Thanks! Really." She whipped out her cell phone. "Here's my number in case you need to reach me for anything."

Wow! Matt had not been expecting the beautiful EMT to offer him her phone number. Not that he was complaining. It was a boost to his sorely damaged ego. He dug for his phone. "I'm ready when you're ready."

She rattled off her number, and he quickly texted her back so she would have his.

"Take care of her for me, will you, Matt?" she pleaded anxiously.

On second thought, there was nothing flirtatious about Star's demeanor. It was entirely possible that their exchange of phone numbers was exactly what she'd claimed it was — a means of staying in touch about the status of her friend's condition. Giving her a reassuring look, Matt fist-bumped her.

Looking grateful, she pushed aside the curtain and was gone. The nurse followed, presumably to report Bree's vitals to the doctor on duty.

Matt moved to the foot of the hospital bed. "So, who do you think I am, Bree?" *And why did you beg me not to leave you?*

Her long blonde lashes remained motionless against her cheeks. It looked like he was going to have to stick around for a while if he wanted answers.

———

Hope you enjoyed this excerpt from
Accidental Hero.
Available in eBook, paperback, hard cover large print, and Kindle Unlimited!

The whole alphabet is coming — read them all!
A - Accidental Hero
B - Best Friend Hero

C - Celebrity Hero

D - Damaged Hero

E - Enemies to Hero

F - Forbidden Hero

G - Guardian Hero

H - Hunk and Hero

I - Instantly Her Hero

J - Jilted Hero

K - Kissable Hero

L - Long Distance Hero

M - Mistaken Hero

N - Not Good Enough Hero

Much love,

Jo

SNEAK PREVIEW: WINDS OF CHANGE

GETTING HIRED *as a high school principal in her hometown is her biggest dream come true, except for one small detail — her ex is the new head of security.*

Ten years ago, Hope Remington graduated with honors from Heart Lake High, while Josh Hawling was…well, bad news on the south side of town. And now she's returning to unite their two rival high schools under one roof. She can't figure out how a guy who spent more time in the principal's office than in class during his teen years managed to convince the school board he can eliminate the student gang problem while coaching a bunch of farm boys into a football team that'll make the playoffs.

Though Hope discovers she feels safer having Josh on their crime-ridden campus, she's still not looking forward to her daily encounters with the cocky head of security. Or being socked in the heart all over again by his devastating smile. Or having to finally face her unwanted attraction to him that might have kindled into a lot more if she'd never left Texas in the first place.

Welcome to Heart Lake! A small town teaming with old family rivalries and the rumble of horses' hooves — faith-filled romance that you'll never forget.

Heart Lake #1: Winds of Change
Available in eBook, paperback, and Kindle Unlimited!

Read them all!
Winds of Change
Song of Nightingales
Perils of Starlight
Return of Miracles
Thousands of Gifts
Race of Champions
Storm of Secrets
Season of Angels
Clash of Hearts
Mountain of Fire

Much love,
Jo

SNEAK PREVIEW: HER BILLIONAIRE BOSS

WHEN THE CEO *of a mega corporation hires the daughter of his family's biggest rival to serve as his personal assistant...*

Jacey Maddox decides to do her part to end her family's decades-old feud with Genesis & Sons by going to work for them. That is, if they'll consider hiring a hated Maddox...

CEO Luca Calcagni is determined to teach the rebel youngest daughter of his family's oldest rival the lesson of her life by agreeing to her foolish request for a job. He gives her a punishing schedule with one goal in mind — to send her running. However, he gets schooled in return when she bravely holds her ground, rekindling his secret attraction to her that he'd mistakenly assumed he was over.

A man known as a cobra in the boardroom isn't supposed to fall for the enemy, and two very powerful families are guaranteed to disapprove if he pursues a second chance at love.

———

Her Billionaire Boss
Available in eBook, paperback, and Kindle Unlimited!

BLACK TIE BILLIONAIRES SERIES
Complete series — read them all!
Her Billionaire Boss
Her Billionaire Bodyguard
Her Billionaire Secret Admirer
Her Billionaire Best Friend
Her Billionaire Geek
Her Billionaire Double Date
Black Tie Billionaires Box Set #1 (Books 1-3)
Black Tie Billionaires Box Set #2 (Books 4-6)

Much love,
Jo

ALSO BY JO GRAFFORD

For the most up-to-date printable list of my books:

Click here

or go to:

https://www.JoGrafford.com/books

For the most up-to-date printable list of books by Jo
Grafford, writing as Jovie Grace *(sweet historical romance)*:

Click here

or go to:

https://www.jografford.com/joviegracebooks

ABOUT JO

Jo is an Amazon bestselling author of sweet and inspirational romance stories about faith, hope, love and family drama with a few Texas-sized detours into comedy.

1.) Follow on Amazon!
amazon.com/author/jografford

2.) Join Cuppa Jo Readers!
https://www.facebook.com/groups/
CuppaJoReaders

3.) Follow on Bookbub!
https://www.bookbub.com/authors/jo-grafford

4.) Follow on YouTube
https://www.youtube.com/channel/
UC3R1at97Qso6BXiBIxCjQ5w

Made in United States
North Haven, CT
17 September 2023

41661036R00150